When A

DCI Dani Bevan #14

The Garansay Press

Books by Katherine Pathak

The Imogen and Hugh Croft Mysteries:

Aoife's Chariot

The Only Survivor

Lawful Death

The Woman Who Vanished

Memorial for the Dead
(Introducing DCI Dani Bevan)

The Ghost of Marchmont Hall

A Better Place

Short Story collection:

The Flawed Emerald and other Stories

DCI Dani Bevan novels:

Against a Dark Sky

On a Dark Sea

A Dark Shadow Falls

Dark as Night

The Dark Fear

Girls of The Dark

Hold Hands in the Dark

Dark Remedies

Dark Origin

The Dark Isle

Dark Enough to See

The Eye in the Dark

The Dark Raven

When All Is Dark

Standalone novels:

I Trust You

#WhenAllIsDark

Edited by: The Currie Revisionists, 2022

Although inspired by real events, the characters and action in this novel are entirely fictitious.
As are the islands of North and South Dorga, which only exist in the author's imagination.

Prologue

A thin layer of snow lay across the fields. The white sprinkling from a brief, overnight blizzard swiftly blown away in the early hours had even topped the grey rocks which marked the jagged headland as it stretched into the North Sea. The lighthouse's fresh coat of blue painted stripes contrasted pleasingly with the white carpet that surrounded it. The sun had just begun to rise behind the old building, bathing it in a golden glow.

The man standing at the sink, gazing out of the narrow window at the view, nodded appreciatively to himself. Trinity House had done a half decent job with that paintwork, he thought idly.

The water that juddered out of the tarnished tap was stained brown, like the freshwater in the burn which trickled beside their house in summer and gushed in winter. He brought a palmful up to splash onto his face and gasped at the harsh cold of it. He knew there'd be a risk of a pipe freezing that night if he wasn't careful to come out and lag the ones which snaked around the outside of the building when he finished work for that day.

He reached for a towel and rubbed his face, dropping it in the laundry basket as he passed the main bedroom, where his wife was still unmoving under the thick duvet. "Time to get up!" He called amiably, adding a knock on both his children's doors to make his point.

The kitchen was icy cold, he turned on the boiler and considered lighting the open fire in the living room to encourage his family to make a start to the day. Since they'd moved here, the cold had been the toughest thing to get used to, or maybe it was the desperately short days in winter, he wasn't sure. But the open space and the peace and quiet had compensated for it. Which didn't mean he wasn't longing for spring.

He filled the kettle and reached into the fridge for the jars of jam and marmalade, along with a pat of butter wrapped in greaseproof paper that Rachel had made herself. As he was placing slices of bread in the toaster, he jerked his head up as there came a sharp knock at the door. He glanced at the clock. It was ten past seven, far too early for Nic to be coming to pick the kids up for school. A frown crinkled his brow.

The knocking came again, it was persistent.

"Who on earth's that?" Rachel's voice travelled down the stairwell; an irritated, sharp tone to it. Reminiscent of mornings when they lived in the city and nerves were always frayed.

He could hear movement upstairs; the sounds of the kids performing their morning routine. He slid back the lock and opened the heavy door, squinting to take in the unusual scene on the path before him. Two policemen in uniform were standing by the gate at the side of the single-track road which passed their property and wound its way to the lighthouse. A couple of women in dark, padded coats were positioned closer, one clutched a clipboard and the other a brand new looking teddy bear with a red bow under her arm. The odd sight made him wonder if he was still dreaming.

A suited man he vaguely recognised pushed forward, shoving a sheet of paper into his hand; full of closely typed script and bearing an official header. He just made out the words, 'place of safety order', before this group of people were suddenly in his house, charging up the stairs.

"What is this?" He called after them in bewilderment.

One of the policemen had remained at the front door. "We've got all the correct paperwork, sir. There's no point in making a fuss. It will only make things worse for you."

He shook his head violently, as if this bizarre early morning invasion of his home could be banished from his mind by force. Rachel had started shouting, it sounded as if she was on the landing. He ran up the stairs.

His wife had their son clasped in her arms, whilst one of the women, still in her thick shapeless coat, was tugging at his arm.

"What in the name of God are you doing!?" He yelled. "Get your hands off my child!"

"It's for his own safety," the woman said levelly. "You need to let him go or the policemen will arrest you both."

He turned towards the suited gentleman, who had averted his gaze to the woodchipped wall. "Why are you trying to take our children? What is happening here?"

"Read the document, it's all in there. The Sheriff's given his orders."

"What *Sheriff*? Who are you talking about?" He gripped his curly fringe as if he might tear the hair straight away from the scalp. Then he looked into the bathroom, where his twelve year old daughter was screaming and squirming, the other woman pulling her by the waist as she gripped the old wash hand basin with both hands. "They don't want to go with you! Can't you see that? What you're doing is assaulting a child!"

"It happens from time to time," the man muttered. "Unpleasant but necessary."

Just as he was about to protest again, there

came an awful wrenching sound. His mouth fell open as he saw that the sink had come away from the wall in a cloud of plaster dust and the icy water from the dislodged pipe was gushing onto the floor tiles, soaking the second woman's sensible shoes.

In the chaos of the moment, his daughter's grip must have loosened because she was abruptly dragged bodily past him and down the stairs. His son, already having been yanked from his mother's arms was being manhandled along the path ahead of his sister. They were all outside in a matter of seconds. The policemen were holding him and his wife back roughly as their children disappeared into the back of a nondescript car.

He must have been shouting, but he couldn't hear anything above the pounding of blood in his ears. The car sped away, despite the terrible, icy conditions. The grip on his body slackened and before the couple could register the departure of the two officers, they were suddenly alone on the front step, the landscape surrounding them deserted, their world a sea of white and grey, except for a discarded teddy bear, lying halfway along the path, the fur still looking pristine and golden, with its red bow like a gash of bright crimson blood.

Chapter 1
Glasgow, 30th October 2021

The radio DJ announced that the early morning mist over the city of Glasgow was due to lift by 9am, revealing a crisp, sunny autumn day. Her perky voice faded out and was replaced by Louis Armstrong crooning about it being a Wonderful World, which DCI Dani Bevan had to acknowledge was an appropriate choice.

Dani sipped her espresso gazing out of the patio doors in the kitchen of her ground floor flat in Scotstounhill. She shuddered as a damp chill seeped through the old rubber strips of insulation surrounding the thin frames. It made her think how they should really be replaced. They must hardly have been energy efficient any longer and had been in place since she'd moved in nearly a decade before.

She felt a presence beside her. James rested his hand on her shoulder. "The calm before the storm, eh?"

Dani turned and smiled. "This is the biggest event the city has ever hosted, certainly the most complex I've ever had to police."

"You've got assistance though, haven't you?" James moved over to the coffee machine to refresh his cup.

Glasgow was to be the venue for the global COP26 climate conference which was running for two weeks and began at 12pm BST that day. But the preparations had begun many months earlier. Dani rinsed her mug under the tap and placed it on the draining board. "We have the security forces accompanying each of the overseas delegates and dozens of additional officers have been brought in from across the country. But if something goes wrong, you can bet your life the buck stops with us."

"The DCC is the one ultimately responsible, though, surely?"

Dani brushed her lips against his warm cheek, smelling his aftershave and the scent of shampoo lingering in his freshly washed hair. "Yes, in theory, but if the Chief Constable wants to find a scapegoat, it will be Ronnie Douglas or me who will be left carrying the can."

"Let's hope it doesn't come to that. You've been planning this operation for over a year. There'll be some grumbling about disruption to the local traffic, but hopefully folk will see this event is far more important than a bit of short term inconvenience."

Dani ran a hand through her shoulder-length hair, lifted her briefcase and slid her feet into a pair of sensible court shoes. "I'm not convinced it is."

James raised his eyebrows. "Don't let the First Minister hear you say that."

Dani grinned. "I wouldn't dream of it. It's just that when you see the lists of delegates and their entourages, printed out endlessly in black and white, you begin to wonder what this diplomatic circus is really all about."

James raised his cup. "We're saving the planet, darling," he replied with more than a hint of irony.

Dani laughed and clipped across the entrance hall to the front door, wondering at what exact point in her career she had become so cynical.

*

The serious crime division of the Pitt Street headquarters was as busy with officers as the DCI had ever seen it. Detective Chief Superintendent Ronnie Douglas was addressing the floor.

Dani checked her watch. It was 10am. She stood beside her superior officer whilst he spoke.

"Now, I don't need to remind you how important the next couple of weeks is going to be for this city and for Police Scotland. Delegates and their security teams will be arriving at the SEC venue from 12 noon today. The traffic division have ensured the M8 exit will be clear for the delegates' convoys to pass through without delays. Local traffic has been diverted along the A8, Paisley Road." Douglas took a breath. "Your responsibility is the policing of the venue itself, alongside your usual duties to patrol the city centre. We already have a team over at the conference centre. DI Muir is leading the operation for the diplomatic division who have seconded him back for the duration of the conference. But the point is, that we must work together on this." He raised a finger to emphasise his words. "You will be patrolling the venues and the streets of Glasgow in a matter of hours. I need you to observe *everything*. Suspect packages, unusual behaviour, suspicious vehicles. Hell, if someone farts in the wrong place during the next two weeks, I want to hear about it."

A murmur of laughter rippled through the group, but Dani noticed many of the officers were too tense to see much humour in the situation.

"DCI Bevan will be here in the department to head up the operation. Pitt Street will be your HQ. We have nearly two hundred world leaders in our fair city from today, including the President of the United States. This will be something you'll tell the grandkids about. But make no mistake, this is the most important assignment of your careers. There'll be no room for errors."

Dani glanced at the roomful of faces, some seemed pumped up for the challenge, others as jaded as they were on any given Monday morning briefing. But a few had paled at the DCS's words, their expressions displaying what could only be described as pure fear at the enormity of the task before them.

After the DCS's pep talk, Dani had divided the officers into sections which all had a commanding officer and a specific set of duties for the following days. This operation had been planned months in advance. She had a smartboard with a spreadsheet showing her where all her officers would be at any given moment in the next two weeks.

They'd tried to model all possible scenarios that might take place, but if the DCI had learnt anything during her career, it was that people were unpredictable. With the number of individuals, from so many interest groups they had gathered in the city right at that moment, the prospect of unwelcome surprises made her distinctly uneasy.

Dani was about to return to her office when DI Alice Mann approached her. "Is everything okay, Alice?"

The young woman nodded assuredly. She had only that month returned from maternity leave. Her little boy was now two and a half years old. But the DI was still on reduced hours. "I'm afraid Fergus is in court all day today. I'm going to have to clock off at 4.30pm to pick up Charlie from nursery."

Dani noticed her colleague's pale face had coloured across the cheeks. It was obvious how much it pained her to ask for this kind of dispensation. But to Dani, it was entirely understandable, she wanted Alice in her team, she was one of the best officers she'd ever worked with. If flexible hours was what it took to keep her, it was a small price to pay. "No problem. Andy is on your team and he has been as thoroughly briefed as you have. When you leave, he can take over command."

Alice's posture relaxed with relief. "Yes, I'll do that. I do know how important these next few weeks are, but Fergus's court date couldn't be shifted."

"Don't explain yourself, Alice. You've a child now and I know things will change. Andy was disgruntled not to get a command, so if he can share yours it may appease him." She sighed, "if he wants greater responsibility, he'll have to take those Inspector exams."

Alice nodded. "We can work together, we've done it plenty of times before. Andy knows the city better than any other officer at Pitt Street."

"He's also got a list of prejudices and gripes as long as the Clyde. If he starts mouthing off, don't hesitate to shut him down. Our presence at this conference is going to be strictly, *seen and not heard*," Dani said with emphasis.

Alice smiled. "Message received, Ma'am." She turned to gather her team, ready for the task ahead.

Chapter 2

The police van crawled along Commercial Street. The eight officers in the back all wore high visibility jackets with Kevlar vests underneath.

The windows had misted up with condensation and Alice felt sweat beginning to bead her brow. “The public shouldn’t be aware of the routes the first delegates are taking to reach the SEC, as a result, many of the protests are taking place in the city centre itself today.”

DS Andy Calder cleared his throat. “Do we have any insider knowledge of where they’re planning to congregate?”

DC Dan Clifton piped up from the seat opposite the DS, “yes, a few of us on the tech team have infiltrated an online forum for the ‘Earth’s Saviours’ group, which have been the most recently active in Scotland. That’s how we know they’re gathering today at Broomielaw Quay.” The young man lifted his chin proudly.

“I wonder how long it will take for them to work out they’ve got a leak and shut the forum down?” Andy added grumpily. “When we keep gate-crashing their party?”

DS Sharon Moffatt, squashed up next to Dan, pulled a face. “Maybe they won’t. The group want maximum publicity, right? I’m sure they’re happily tipping off the press about where they’ll be. It’s been a pattern for all their previous protests.”

“That’s right,” DC Calvin added from his place by the rear doors, “Earth’s Saviours have already protested at Central Station in August this year. A number of their members climbed on top of an LNER train. The press arrived within minutes and the pictures were being broadcast around the world by lunchtime. It's generating publicity for their aims that motivates them."

"The train should have pulled out of the station with them still on top," Andy muttered under his breath.

Alice heard him. "I hope that's just a poor taste joke, DS Calder. Legitimate, peaceful protest is entirely legal in this country. Our role is to make sure it stays peaceful. Any prejudices, we leave at home." She gave her colleague a cold stare.

Andy shrugged his broad shoulders. He knew he'd have to keep his opinions to himself for these two weeks. If it was up to him, Glasgow would never have hosted this *climate* conference. It wasn't that he didn't think climate change was going on. Of course he did; he, Cathy and Amy were lazing on the beach at Largs in nearly 30 degree heat that summer. It was just the hypocrisy he couldn't stomach; the lines of gas guzzling diesels dropping off the troops of delegates, the private school educated grungies gluing themselves to the types of transport the First Minister was always telling them was eco-friendly. Andy was old enough to remember the proud steelworkers and shipbuilding industry that flourished along the Clyde, now vilified as a symbol of a shameful, fossil-fuel centred past.

DC Tait nudged Andy's arm. The van had stopped and his team were jumping out of the rear doors into the welcome cold but fresh air of the north bank of the Clyde.

The protestors were immediately visible. They had picketed the road and were maybe a couple of hundred in number. They had dressed in green smocks and held placards with slogans cheerfully predicting the climate apocalypse in bright daubs of paint. One eye-catching banner was held by several hands in fingerless, knitted gloves, spread across the frontline of the protest, just metres away from them. It was professionally printed and stated, "Keep To The Limit of 1.5 Degrees!" In a bright green against a red background.

Alice knew this was a message for the COP26 delegates, delivered to them via the media. The very minimum that the climate action groups had recommended ahead of this conference was a target to limit global warming emissions to 1.5 degrees above pre-industrial levels. These protesters were here to ensure the leaders from the developed world didn't backtrack on this pledge. Unlike Andy, the DI had sympathy for their view. She had Charlie now and wanted the world to be protected for his sake. Governments had to act decisively now to stop the crisis getting worse.

The TV crews and newspaper hacks were already congregating on the banks of the quay. Alice knew it would make their day to be able to capture trouble breaking out between the protestors and the police. Conflict was meat and drink to them. It was the DI's job to make sure there was nothing of interest to report on BBC Scotland at 6pm.

Her team had already formed their protective line along the riverbank pavement just to the side of the protestors, showing their presence, but without appearing confrontational. It was a formation they'd modelled many times.

Alice fell in beside Andy. "It seems peaceful. They aren't looking ready to move anytime soon. There's a group over there cracking open flasks of tea."

Andy managed a smile. "Not the most intimidating villains we've ever faced."

"Although, both you and I know how quickly these situations can turn nasty if a militant element show up."

He nodded his agreement, gazing over at the rag-tag group of protestors. Most were in homemade looking green smocks, carrying placards with slogans like; 'the Earth is dying,' slapped on with paint. But others were carrying tall wooden crosses which had the appearance of two strips of plywood nailed together. Andy pointed at the symbols. "Is there a religious element to this group?"

It was DS Sharon Moffett who answered, "they call themselves, 'Earth's Saviours', when of course, in Christianity, the saviour of man was Jesus Christ. They are a secular group that see themselves as saviours of the planet instead, but they use the symbol of the cross as it represents both sacrifice and re-birth."

Andy cast her a querying glance.

"I actually did my homework DS Calder," she replied cheerfully.

"I must have missed that assignment," he replied grumpily.

"Actually, I asked Sharon specifically to look into 'Earth's Saviours' and their aims. She did an extremely thorough job," Alice explained.

Andy watched the strange procession of tall crosses bobbing up and down within the crowd, an odd contrast against the industrial frontages of the old wharf. "They must piss off the religious types then, even though they're eco-warriors and all that?"

"Yes, they definitely do," Sharon explained. "The use of the crucifixion cross has been condemned by the Scottish church, who sympathise with the cause, but want the symbol dropped. They had a lively discussion about it on 'Debate Night' last week. The Moderator of the Church of Scotland took part."

As the officers contemplated this, a woman broke free of the crowd and headed towards them. She was dressed in corduroy dungarees with a green tabard covering her thin frame. Her hair was styled in long dread-locks but her face was as pale as the cloudy sky. "I'm Macy McAdams, the leader of Earth's Saviours in Glasgow. I thought I'd introduce myself."

Alice stepped forward. "DI Mann, the officer in charge. We hope this afternoon can remain peaceful."

The woman's expression was steely. "We are a peaceful group, but when the Earth is under attack, we will not hesitate to defend it."

Not quite sure what this meant, Alice was determined to remain diplomatic. "Are you planning to move anywhere else today?"

"Yes, at 4.30pm we are going to cross the Kingston Bridge. We know most of the delegates will be transported to the south of the river, as the conference centre is located there, so we want to get as close as possible, so our message reaches the right people."

Alice cursed under her breath, she had to pick Charlie up from nursery at 5pm. "If you give us some prior notice and a provisional route we can alert our officers down there as to your arrival time."

"Co-operating with the police?" Her scrubbed, un-made up face broke into a mocking smile. "We couldn't have that now, could we?" The woman turned and marched back to the protest, where she was quickly absorbed into the crowd.

"I've got a feeling these people are going to seriously piss me off after a while," Andy muttered into the collar of his jacket.

For once, Alice completely agreed with her second in command.

"I think that's the point, Andy," Sharon retorted, giving her colleague a friendly shove.

Andy didn't reply, but strengthened his stance,

scanning the crowd for even the slightest sign of trouble.

Chapter 3

Scraps of paper were beginning to overload Dani's usually tidy desk. Complaints were flooding into the switchboard and it was only day two of the conference. Most of them were about road closures and diversions around the city centre. People had been encouraged to avoid the area as much as possible, but Dani knew there was always a significant group who would insist on ploughing on as usual.

She pushed the pile to the side and approached the smartboard, examining the itinerary for the day. Elon Musk was due to address the conference at 2pm. Dani knew he had his own private protection team and that the security at the centre was rock solid. Her concern were the roads and bridges that surrounded it.

Dani dragged a hand through her shoulder-length, chestnut brown hair. The concern for her wasn't really the protests. Alice and Andy had reported no issues from their assignment the previous day. Disruption she was expecting. The cause of the niggling sense of dread that had settled in her stomach since the conference began, was the ever-present fear of a terrorist attack. The threat could potentially come from any unassuming vehicle in the vicinity of the SEC; a work van or taxi, or even an anonymous, nondescript member of the public. The anti-terrorist squad had reported no particular spike of activity amongst the networks they observed, but these were still the worries that kept her up at night.

There was a knock at the door. DCS Ronnie Douglas entered, handing her a take-out cup of black coffee.

"Thank you sir." She noted his face was drawn with concern and his mouth turned down at the corners. "Is there a problem?"

"Have you been receiving complaints from the public?"

Dani dipped her head towards the messy pile on her desk. "Dozens, mostly from disgruntled motorists, and a good number from those angered at their appointments at the Infirmary being cancelled or postponed."

Douglas nodded. "My secretary has had plenty of those too. But we received an email this morning which is of even greater concern. The Women's Association of Scotland have lodged an official complaint against Police Scotland."

Dani took a gulp of her bitter drink, dreading what was coming, sensing it was going to be out of leftfield.

"Apparently, a number of their members have been in touch with them. Due to our road closures, many local woman are having to find different routes to walk home through."

Dani took a deep breath, her brain quickly joining the dots. "We've closed off all the main, well-lit highways, leaving the locals to find their way home from work and school along dark, lonely routes, across parks maybe, when the sun is setting at 4.30pm. Shit. How did I miss this?"

"Because we had a thousand other remits we had to follow. Because the entire idea of hosting an international conference in a busy, compact city like Glasgow, with a history as a soft terrorist target was complete madness." He managed a pained smile. "Because we are always being tasked with the impossible, and rather too often, you and your team deliver it."

Dani sank into one of her soft chairs. "But this is

different. I pride myself on putting the vulnerable first, it's been a hallmark of my career." She waved a hand at her detailed, colour-co-ordinated smartboard. "I've been spending every waking hour making the city safe for men in suits, who sit in cars with armoured glass, surrounded by an entourage of bodyguards. Did I think enough about the ordinary citizens of Glasgow?"

Douglas took the chair opposite. "We've been given a wake-up call, Dani. That email I received was a warning. Those women have complained, as well they might, but nobody has been attacked yet. We've got a chance to put things right, so we do it, and fast."

Dani felt the jolt of caffeine reaching her system, jumping to her feet. "You're right. It's Day 2 and there's time to sort this out. I'll re-deploy a team to create a system of safer routes for pedestrians around the city. We can make sure the information hits the media before dusk today. God knows, we won't have this kind of budget to play with again."

The DCS rose more slowly from his seat. "Good. It will be something to tell the Women's Association when I call the Chief Secretary. But I'll have to inform the DCC of the complaint. I expect he'll be required to make an apology on the six o'clock news."

Dani could see the strain in her superior's face. For once, she didn't envy him his position, not at all.

Chapter 4

The woman pulled her hood up to cover her neatly plaited hair and headed out into the rain. Her low heels clicked against the pavement as she fell into her usual rhythm, making her way home to her flat in Gallowgate.

A crumpled sheet of paper was gripped in her hand. She lifted it up to check the directions printed on it. She'd downloaded it from the BBC website at work after receiving an email from the women's group she was a member of which had recommended it.

The previous evening, she had found the London Road completely closed. Instead, she had been required to walk an extra couple of miles to find a dark side street which ran along beside the old railway line and brought her out on the industrial estate. She reached home eventually, but her heart was pounding in her chest for the entire journey, her ears alert for the sounds of footsteps behind her.

Now, she noted that a brightly lit pedestrian walkway had been created past Celtic Park. As she approached, it became clear that police officers had been stationed at regular intervals along it. She glanced back at the sheet in her hand, the ink becoming smudged by the relentless drizzle, thinking she'd laminate it in the office the next morning.

The website had made reference to the officer who had devised the plan, one of the only female DCIs in Scotland. The name had stuck in her mind because it was like the man who had been in charge of the miners during the war. Her grandfather had been one of those. A Bevin Boy. But this name was spelt with an 'a'. The reporter had even referred to these diversions as the 'Bevan routes'. So it would be hard for her to forget that name.

The woman lifted her head and smiled at one of the uniformed officers from beneath her hood. He smiled reassuringly back. She continued on her way, thankful that during the chaos of the climate conference which everyone in her office was moaning about, this Bevan woman had made her day so much easier.

*

The rich smell of pan-frying meat floated down the hallway as Dani leant against the wall to kick off her shoes. She shrugged out of her suit jacket and placed it on a hook.

"I'm doing venison steaks, if that's okay," James called from the kitchen. "Apparently, it's incredibly good for the environment to help keep the Scottish deer population down by eating their locally sourced meat."

Dani slid onto one of the chairs at her small kitchen table, stretching out her stockinged feet with a sigh. "Poor deer. Another victim of the latest climate-saving fad. Time to cull Bambi."

James laughed, pouring her a glass of red. "I know you don't really mean that," he added. "I take it running an international climate conference is taking its toll on your nerves, darling?"

She reached out for the glass and took a generous mouthful. The wine was smooth with hints of nuttiness, she knew it would perfectly complement the venison. "Did you see the six o'clock news?"

"I certainly did. Sally was on the phone straight after. She's hugely impressed. She wants to know if they can have some 'Bevan routes' in Edinburgh."

"I would have accepted her admiration gladly if I'd actually come up with the idea ahead of the conference, not when I was simply responding to the complaints of dozens of poor women forced to walk home along dark, lonely alleyways at night."

James flipped the steaks, a pan of new potatoes boiled on the adjacent hob, a simple salad stood in an earthenware bowl on the countertop. The sizzling sound made Dani's mouth water and her stomach contract. She'd not eaten since breakfast, trying to sort out last-minute policing for her 'safe pedestrian routes' for the entire day.

He turned back to face her. "That's how new developments are made. Someone points out the flaws in your plan and you make the appropriate changes as quickly as possible. That's exactly what you did. So stop beating yourself up. This whole conference seems to going rather smoothly if you ask me, according to the media reports, anyway."

Dani took another slug of wine. She knew her boyfriend meant well, but she wished he hadn't tempted fate with those words he'd just spoken. "Let's try those steaks then. I'm absolutely starving."

James's face lit up and he gathered up a couple of plates. "Coming right up, madam. Just as you like it, medium rare?"

"As long as Bambi isn't going to suddenly jump up and start frolicking around the room, I'm easy."

Chapter 5

The dark suit jacket strained over DI Dermot Muir's Kevlar vest and communications equipment. It was nearly a year since he'd last had to wear it. He decided to stop accepting the packet of fresh doughnuts DS Moffett insisted on placing on his desk each morning. He was getting seriously out of shape.

Dermot made sure his earpiece was firmly in place and scanned the vast conference room from his position by the entrance doors. The US president and UK Prime Minister had left Glasgow at 9am that morning. He had been in the close-ops team which accompanied the president to his car. For the first time in many months, he'd felt the weight of a government issue gun in a holster against his chest and the adrenaline rush of a top security assignment.

It made the DI wonder for a while why he'd ever left this line of work. But now he was back in the conference hall, he remembered why he'd sought the transfer to the SCD under DCI Bevan. Most of the time, the work of the diplomatic corps was like that of a glorified club bouncer, but with better dressed clientele to protect.

Whereas, since he'd been at Pitt Street, he had been able to properly exercise his detecting skills, using his brain for once. It had been remarkably refreshing.

Dermot checked his Omega Speed Master watch, an overly extravagant gift from his ex-fiancé. It was nearly lunchtime. He and his colleagues would escort the delegates into the canteen shortly. Now that the world leaders were heading home, the real negotiations would begin in the smaller conference rooms which were dotted about the modern complex. Discussions would stretch into the early hours between the representatives of all the participating countries and various business leaders and scientists. The DI was reluctant to tempt fate, but this should have meant the threat level diminished from this point onwards, even though his hours spent on duty would remain long.

The future pressure points were when major media figures such as Sir David Attenborough and Greta Thunberg arrived to give talks to the delegates. But without the world leaders present, it still felt as if a certain amount of weight had been lifted from Dermot's shoulders, especially when he got confirmation in his earpiece that the president's plane had taken off from Glasgow airport and was now somewhere over the Atlantic Ocean.

Dermot's security team were to take their lunch when the delegates had finished theirs and returned to the afternoon programme of debates. The DI placed his tray next to an old colleague of his called DS Ronan Quirke. They exchanged news over a plateful of chicken salad. If Ronan was surprised to hear Dermot was no longer engaged to be married, the officer didn't show it. He was too pre-occupied with the strains of having a new baby in the house he shared with his wife alongside the unpredictable hours required by the diplomatic service.

Dermot was about to suggest maybe his friend should consider a transfer himself when an officer from another team strode into the canteen and approached their table. Something about the man's pinched expression made Dermot put down his fork without tasting the food balanced on it.

"I'm stationed at Conference Room 12, second floor east. According to the secretary, one of the delegates hasn't returned after lunch. A man called,

Quentin Lester, 58 years old. Is he still in here, finishing his lunch, maybe?" The officer cast an eye about the room.

Dermot and his team were immediately on their feet. The guy was probably in a men's toilet somewhere, but they couldn't afford to be complacent.

"There's nobody except us left in here," Dermot said. "We should check the public bathrooms on this floor and the one above. Congregate back in the foyer when we're done."

The others nodded their agreement and abandoned their lunches without demur.

*

When Dermot and the rest of his team re-assembled in the huge, light-filled foyer of the SEC, they were all shaking their heads.

"No sign of the delegate on the first or second floor," Dermot spoke into his headset.

Within seconds, the officer who had approached them in the canteen came jogging down the stairs. "He's still not turned up for the meeting in Room 12."

"Is there somewhere designated for delegates to go for a fag between sessions?" DS Quirke suggested, not wishing to call in back-up until they'd covered all possibilities.

"There's a balcony on each floor set aside as smoking areas. I've already checked the one nearest the conference room. It was empty," the officer explained.

Dermot puffed himself up. "Right, he's now been unaccounted for," he glanced at his watch, "for roughly half an hour. It's time to widen the search. We've been told to look out for *anything* unusual. The man could've bunked off for a shopping trip to the St Enoch Centre, but it doesn't matter, we need to treat this as high priority."

*

Dani Bevan had just come off the phone from a call with Dermot Muir. Her DI was seconded to the diplomatic division for the following two weeks but was urgently requesting information about a Scottish delegate to the conference named Quentin Lester.

She popped her head out of the door of her office and scanned the room. Most of her teams were out patrolling the city or the SEC. She spotted DC Sullivan seated at his workstation, immediately calling him over.

The young DC entered the office behind his boss. "How can I help, Ma'am?"

The DCI gestured to the smartboard. "A security team have noticed that one of the delegates, a Quentin Lester, hasn't returned to meetings after lunch. It could be nothing, but we need to track him down, fast." She pointed to a column of names. "According to the automated register, Lester attended the lecture on 'Global Warming and the Oceans', in the main hall this morning."

"How does the register work, Ma'am?"

"All delegates are required to scan their ID cards upon entry to each meeting or seminar, which they are wearing on lanyards. The delegates know how important security is at the conference and have been very diligent at clocking in and out. By ten past one, a secretary noticed this Lester chap hadn't arrived back from lunch. A preliminary search was conducted, but he hasn't been found yet."

"Anyone claim to have seen him at lunch?"

Dani thought this was a good question. "The security team haven't had time to interview fellow delegates yet. I've informed DI Muir of Lester's hotel and room number, which I have held here for all the delegates and speakers. He's staying at the Holiday Lodge Express on the southside."

Sullivan nodded. "I know where it is."

Dani sighed. "We're low on manpower here at the station, so I want you to find out everything there is to know about Quentin Lester. Who does he work for, what are his likes, dislikes and prejudices? I know it's a big ask for you to take on single-handed. But if it turns out this guy has slipped through the vetting system somehow, we need to know about it. Right now."

The DC remained reassuringly calm. "I'll get onto it straightaway, Ma'am."

Chapter 6

The Holiday Lodge Express was quiet at this time of the day. Dermot knew most of its guests were attending the conference and wouldn't be back until after the evening meal was served at the SEC canteen.

In fact, he had to bang on a few doors to find the member of staff who was supposed to be on the reception desk. He made a mental note to tell his next-in-command. These hotels were making big money from the conference, the least they could do was to make sure they had staff noting who came in and out.

The DI had brought DS Quirke with him. The rest of the team were searching the lanes and gardens surrounding the SEC, in the hope their missing man was having a sneaky fag and a takeout coffee on a bench somewhere.

The receptionist tapped at the keypad in front of her with long, painted nails which seemed to make the process ten times harder. She stared at the computer screen. "Mr Lester checked in on Wednesday at 4pm, along with the majority of other guests attending the conference."

"Yes, but what about today?" He was trying to keep the irritation out of his voice. "Did he come down for the hotel breakfast?"

She nodded her head of dark brown hair. "Yes, it seems his room number was ticked off for the complimentary breakfast this morning at 7.45am."

"Okay. Has he returned to his room since then?" Dermot already feared he knew the answer to this question.

She made eye-contact, her face slick with freshly applied make-up. "Mr Lester has his own key card, Officer. He can come and go as he pleases."

“So have you had anyone come back to the hotel from the conference today? Around lunchtime maybe?”

She had the decency to look abashed. “I’m not sure I would have noticed. I haven’t been on the desk the entire time.”

Dermot breathed away a reprimand. This woman wasn’t a member of his team. It wasn’t his place to criticise her work practices. “We are going to need to gain entry to his room.”

For a moment, she seemed to hesitate. “I’ll be required to call the manager, but I can certainly give you the spare key card now.”

Dermot took the card with what he hoped was a grateful smile, but what he suspected appeared more like a grimace.

*

The hotel corridors all looked identical. They stopped outside the room number the receptionist had given them. Dermot knocked loudly on the door.

“Mr Lester! Are you inside?” He didn’t wait long for an answer, feeling enough time had already been wasted at the front desk.

He slotted the card into the casing fixed by the door and pulled down the handle as the green light came on. The first thing that struck the detective was the odd smell. It was very warm in the room and the curtains had been drawn. An metallic aroma filled his nostrils. He knew what that smell indicated. He turned to his companion and lowered his voice. “Don’t touch anything, Ronan.”

The other man nodded with a weary understanding.

“Mr Lester,” Dermot continued to call. “Are you okay?”

They were greeted with silence, but as Dermot took a couple of steps into the room and was able to fully survey the scene, his legs nearly gave way beneath him. He heard Ronan gasp.

The curtains were thin and cheap, allowing them to see the tableau quite clearly. A man was sprawled out on the bed, a type of academic gown hung loosely around his shoulders over a blood-stained shirt. His trousers and underpants had been pulled off completely, leaving only the socks on his feet. In the centre of his chest was embedded a simple wooden cross. Dermot estimated it was maybe two feet high and one across. It seemed homemade, there were unevenly secured screws visible where the two strips of wood met.

The DI wondered if the end of the cross had been sharpened to a point, as it appeared to have entered the chest cleanly. There was less blood seeping from the wound than he might have expected, so the object had most likely penetrated deep into the chest cavity.

“Is he still alive?” Ronan’s voice was a rasp. “There isn’t much blood?”

Dermot looked at the man’s face. It was deathly white and the blank eyes were staring open at the ceiling. He took one more step forward and touched the wrist of a hand dangling off one side of the bed, careful not to disturb anything else. The skin was cold, but rigor had certainly not set in yet. He turned and shook his head. He searched the small room with his eyes, craning his neck round the door of the bathroom. The perpetrator was long gone.

“We need to leave now. Then I’ll call it in. If I deal with the serious crime division, can you liaise with the security team? They can call off the search.”

Ronan reached for his radio without delay.

Dermot glanced back into the room briefly, noticing the man’s briefcase still resting against the side of the bed and his mobile phone placed on the dressing table, before ushering his colleague out into the corridor. Of all the scenarios they'd modelled for these past few months, in preparation for the global conference, this situation certainly wasn't one of them.

Chapter 7

DCS Ronnie Douglas was addressing the room. After he received the call from Bevan, they swiftly decided who they should recall from their patrolling duties to deal with the murder investigation that had been presented to them. They couldn't afford to leave any corner of the city unprotected. But at the same time, solving murders was their raison d'ĕtre.

Dani stood by his side. She'd suggested they bring DI Alice Mann back to the station to head up the investigation, with DS Calder remaining in the field to take full charge of her team. Following a few feverish phone calls to the central division, she was able to bring in several reinforcements, which meant she could also ask Sharon Moffett and Dan Clifton to join the murder team, alongside DC Tyler Sullivan, who had already impressed her with his work. DI Muir would also be returning to them for the foreseeable future. He had a head start on the case and was still at the crime scene with the SOCOs and the city pathologist.

Douglas switched on the smartboard which had been wheeled out of Dani's office onto the main floor of the division, a passport sized image of the head and shoulders of a man with receding grey hair filled the screen. It had been blown up in size, making the features a soft blur. "Our victim, is a 58 year old man called Quentin Lester, from Stirling. We have so far identified him from the testimony of the Holiday Lodge receptionist and the photograph on his ID card, reproduced here. We are still searching for a next of kin." He glared at DC Sullivan. "I believe you have some more detailed information on this man, Sullivan? Share it with us."

The DC took a deep breath, getting to his feet. "Quentin Laws Lester worked for the Global Fund for

Child Welfare as an analyst. They have an office in Grey's Square in Stirling. He was attending COP26 as a delegate for the charity and had been in Glasgow since the event began on Wednesday."

DCS Douglas barked, "what sort of work was he doing for the charity?"

Tyler Sullivan reddened but carried on. "From what I could tell by speaking with their Chief Executive, he gathered and analysed data on factors affecting children's welfare worldwide. This includes the impact of pandemics, economic fluctuations and climate change."

Dani nodded with understanding. "Which explains what he was doing at the conference."

Alice Mann stepped forward. "Our victim sounds like a tiny cog in the wheel of this conference. He was a pen-pusher, an analyst for a charity nobody's heard of. I can't see him being targeted by any terrorist or environmental group?"

Douglas crossed his arms over his broad chest. "I spoke with the First Minister this morning. She has decided, that although a tragic incident, the discovery of Lester's body shouldn't cause any disruption to the conference. As you say, Alice, this hardly seems like a major attack on COP26. The world leaders have already left, so the security risk has been downgraded." He frowned. "From what DI Muir has already told me about the crime scene, we could be looking at an odd sexual encounter gone wrong. It may have nothing to do with the conference at all."

Dani took up the mantle. "Which means that we are to investigate this murder as we usually would, but for the duration of the conference, we keep as much information out of the media as possible. There can be no leaks."

"Something always gets out, Ma'am," Dan Clifton

added philosophically.

"Yes, it does. But don't let the source be any of you lot. *Understood.*"

A ripple of nods greeted her words. The sound of the lift rumbling to a stop on the serious crime floor broke the tense silence.

Dermot Muir emerged from the sliding doors, still dressed in his dark suit and Kevlar vest, he seemed beefier and more intimidating than any of his colleagues had seen him before.

"Ah, DI Muir," Douglas boomed. "You're just in time to talk us through the crime scene."

"I can do better than that," he declared, waving a small memory stick at the team.

*

DS Sharon Moffett watched her colleague closely. Dermot had removed his jacket and unclipped the bullet-proof vest. He seemed much more like the man she knew without the bulky gear.

The memory stick he had inserted into the computer contained the crime scene photos. Dermot had rushed them over as soon as the SOCOs and the pathologist had completed the initial examination of the hotel room.

Sharon stared at the photograph of the corpse. The victim's middle-aged nakedness below the waist, framed by the academic gown, did indeed give the impression of some kind of sexual role-play game gone wrong. His socks were still in place. Wasn't it an old joke that men kept their socks on during sex? She wouldn't know, it was so long since she'd had any herself.

But the general impression of kinky sex was undermined by the sight of the weapon protruding from Lester's chest. Sharon had spent several hours that week researching just such symbols. The significance certainly wasn't lost on her. She raised her hand.

A fleeting look of irritation passed across Dermot's face. "What is it Sharon?"

"I don't know if Alice or Dan have noticed, but that wooden cross looks very much like the ones the Earth's Saviours group were carrying on their protest march yesterday."

Douglas uncrossed his arms. "The environmentalist group?"

Sharon nodded. "I researched them for Alice. They make the crosses themselves and parade them on marches. The cross represents the idea of their group as a 'saviour' of the planet; like Christ saved mankind through the crucifixion." She tried to ignore the disbelieving look that Dermot was giving her.

Alice Mann piped up. "Sharon is right. We saw those crosses everywhere at the Broomielaw Quay demo yesterday. They looked like they'd been hand built, with a couple of strips of plywood and a few screws."

Dermot zoomed in on the weapon shown on screen. "The cross used to stab Lester also looked scratch built. I suspect the end had been sharpened by hand for the purpose, but we won't know until the pathologist removes it, which he is going to do at the *post mortem* later today with any luck."

Dani furrowed her brow. "I'll call the lab later to make sure the *PM* and the forensic analysis of the scene are top priority. We need a result on this as quickly as possible, particularly as the First Minister is observing our progress. At least I've got a big name to throw about to get our results fast-tracked."

"Good, get onto that now will you, Danielle?" Douglas rubbed his rough chin. "Could it be possible that this man was killed by a member of Earth's Saviours? Was he in some way creating opposition to their aims? I would have thought his work would have made him sympathetic to halting climate change. But this 'cross' business puts a different spin on things."

Dermot crinkled his brow in thought. "Alice, we're going to have to question the organisers of Earth's Saviours; find out their movements yesterday and today. See if any of them have had prior dealings with our victim."

Alice nodded. "Dan and Tyler can examine the background of the victim, try to identify a next of kin and home address. I'd like Sharon to work with me, looking into the significance of the dressing of the murder scene and this possible link to Earth's Saviours."

"Right, let's get on with it," Dermot said impatiently. He snatched the memory stick from out of the laptop socket and strode towards his desk. He was eager to return to the intellectual puzzle of solving a murder case, he'd missed it, he realised. His adrenaline was already pumping. He was suddenly put in no doubt that the life of a detective was certainly the one for him.

Chapter 8

The wind was blowing a few stray scraps of litter around the car park of the head office of the Global Fund for Child Welfare. Tyler Sullivan had been to Stirling a couple of times, mostly to see bands gigging at the university. He gazed up at the imposing stone building, which was as grey as the name of the square it sat in.

Dan Clifton climbed the step and pressed a buzzer above a grill. An electronic beep indicated they should enter through the front door. The offices were on the first floor. Despite the austere exterior, the interior of the charity headquarters was modern and bright.

A young man on the reception desk examined their identification cards and indicated they should take the pair of soft chairs in the foyer to wait for assistance. They didn't have to wait for long.

A woman in her mid-fifties approached the detectives. Her hair was a silver-grey and worn in a layered, shoulder-length style. Her expression was pinched with concern.

Dan got to his feet. "Mrs Meakin? We spoke on the phone earlier. I'm DC Clifton and this is DC Sullivan."

"You'd better come into my office," she said by way of reply, resignation in her tone.

The office had a tall casement window which faced the square. The morning sun spilled through its original panes, slicing across the oak desk which was devoid of clutter.

The detectives sat in the chairs opposite the chief executive of the charity. "We still haven't been able to contact a next-of-kin for Mr Lester. This needs to be done as a matter of urgency. He has not so far been identified by the press, but it won't be long until those details will need to be shared publicly. Until then, we will need to rely on your absolute discretion on the matter."

"Of course, detective. I won't notify his colleagues of his death until you give me permission. He was due to be away until the end of the conference anyway. He won't be missed." Mrs Meakin shook her head sadly. "Quentin had been with us for four years. Before that time he worked for an education charity in Africa. In fact, he had worked in the charitable sector ever since completing his Sociology degree at the University of the Highlands in Inverness, sometime in the eighties. His current address is in Fallin; an old pit village to the east of the city. I've never been there myself, we didn't know one another well enough. My understanding is that Quentin lived there alone, although he once mentioned a couple of children from a previous marriage?"

"Yes, we are looking into that," Dan explained. "We will want to examine the property whilst we are here."

"I can certainly provide you with an address, but we don't hold keys or anything like that."

"His belongings were in the hotel room. We are in possession of the keys to his property."

She tutted. "So, it wasn't a burglary then? Quentin wasn't targeted for his credit cards and so forth?"

Dan knew his boss wouldn't be happy if he speculated with this woman about the motive for the crime. "We are still looking into every possibility, Ma'am. Could you tell us more about Mr Lester? What specific employment did he have before coming here?"

She slid on a pair of designer reading glasses and

turned her attention to the computer on the desk. "Quentin came to us from a youth charity operating in Tanzania. He had been based in the capital, Dodoma, for a few years. The charity raised funds to build schools in remote villages. Quentin had been a fundraiser and administrator."

Dan raised his eyebrows. "Okay, so he had spent several years abroad before coming back to Scotland?"

"Yes, I sensed he'd had a difficult divorce and wished to get away for a while. Quentin had been working in the charitable sector for just under thirty years, most of his work had been in Scotland and in the area of education. He had a great deal of experience to bring to his job as analyst for our global fund. That's why I chose him to represent us at COP26. His experience of working abroad was also a bonus."

"Can you think of any reason why someone would want him dead?" Dan knew as he asked the question he was clutching at straws.

Mrs Meakin took off her glasses and rubbed the bridge of her nose. "Quentin was a quiet man. He performed his job diligently and efficiently. I don't believe he had many friends in the office, not beyond polite conversation anyway. We have no complaints lodged against him on his HR file. I'd go as far as to say he was an exemplary employee. The last person you would ever expect to meet a violent end."

"Did you like him personally?" Tyler asked this question, feeling the woman seated before them was giving them the purely professional feedback on Lester.

She thought about this for a moment. "When you informed me he was dead, I was shocked, of course and very saddened. But I wasn't upset. That may sound callous, but I think it's because I don't believe

I really knew the man that well. Not even after four years of his working here."

Dan nodded with understanding. "Thank you for your honesty. If you could provide us with Lester's personnel file now, and let us take a look at his desk, we can leave you in peace."

Chapter 9

Fallin was a neat little village on a bend in the River Forth, a couple miles out of Stirling. The detectives had pulled up beside a semi-detached house of brown pebble-dash with a rusty-red tiled roof.

"It's a pretty modest property," Tyler commented, staring out of the passenger window at the quiet street.

"Lester has lived here for three years. There's a small mortgage on it, but not much, according to his bank details. But then, his salary from the charity was modest too." Dan reached for the set of keys he'd been given by the forensics department after they had analysed them for prints and DNA, finding nothing present but Lester's own.

Tyler slipped on the pair of latex gloves Dan handed him. This property wasn't a crime scene that they knew of, so this was the only protection they would require.

Dan turned the Yale key in the lock. The door needed forcing open against the pile of mail on the mat. "He's only been away a few days," Dan commented under his breath. "Bloody junk mail."

The hallway was dark and lined with old fashioned prints of the Scottish hills and glens. The carpet was swirled with flower patterns and Dan got the sudden sense that Lester hadn't done anything to the interior of this property since he'd moved in three years previously. It seemed to reflect an older woman's taste.

The kitchen was old-fashioned but neat and tidy. The cupboards held just enough crockery and utensils for a single occupant. Pinned to a cork board on the wall beside the fridge were a number of business cards; for taxi firms and takeaway restaurants, all in the Fallin area.

Dan decided to divide the search. He told Tyler to examine the ground floor of the property whilst he took the upstairs. The DC knew that if there were documents and letters to be found which gave them a better insight into the life of their victim, it would be located in the bedroom or study.

The upper floor of the house had a similar feel to downstairs. The rooms were tidy and clean. Dan wondered if Lester had employed a cleaner. If he had they probably didn't yet know the man was dead. They would also contribute another set of prints to the house that would require elimination at some future stage.

The bedroom suggested a single resident. There was a neatly made double bed, but the small table holding a lamp and pile of books sat on one side only. Dan opened the top drawer and dropped the thin selection of postcards and letters it contained into an evidence bag.

The detective noticed no framed photographs on display. He went to the wardrobe, knelt down and scanned the floor for storage boxes. As he suspected, a battered old black concertina style cardboard case was pushed to the back, covered in a layer of dust. He dragged it out. This would be coming back to Pitt Street with them, to add to the box of belongings they had taken from Lester's desk at the charity offices.

Tyler's lanky frame filled the doorway. "I'm finished downstairs," he explained. "There's only really two rooms to search and the guy clearly didn't possess much stuff."

"No, he doesn't seem to have. I've gathered a few personal papers, we can go through them back at the station. Let's have a look in the loft and then see if there's a garage or shed to be found. There are several keys on that keyring of his. Once we've done that, we can call it a day."

*

Dan had just pulled the front door shut, making sure Tyler had all the evidence piled in his arms, when a woman appeared on the step beside them. She looked to be in her late thirties and wore a chequered shirt and jeans. "May I ask what you're doing in Mr Lester's property?"

The detective got out his warrant card and showed it to her. "Have you been Mr Lester's neighbour for long?" He asked.

She furrowed her brow, shaking her mane of sandy blonde hair. "He's only lived there a couple of years. But he's always polite and dead quiet. He's never complained about the noise my kids make and by God, he'd have good reason." She tipped her head curiously. "Is everything alright with him? We've not seen him in a few days now?"

Dan gave a reassuring smile. "Nothing for you to worry about, *Mrs* - ?"

"*Miss* Turnbull. My Kris and I aren't married."

"When did you last see Mr Lester?"

She wrinkled her nose. "It must have been bin day last week, so Tuesday morning. Saw him rolling his wheelie down the drive. I don't think his car has been here since."

"Does he receive many visitors?"

She looked suspicious. "Not a soul, except the cleaner, comes in on a Friday morning. Hey, are you sure he's okay?"

Dan thanked the woman for her help and proceeded down the driveway to where the squad car was parked.

Tyler pulled the passenger door open. "She'll find

out soon enough he's been murdered."

"Yes, but we don't want to be responsible for the story getting out, do we? You remember what Bevan said in the briefing. Besides, it's not like they're at any risk here in Fallin. The murder took place miles away."

Tyler reached across to secure his belt. "You couldn't find a more unassuming house in a more unassuming street. It certainly feels many miles from that creepy murder scene."

Dan eased the car out onto the deserted road, not even needing to use his indicator, thinking how right his young colleague was.

Chapter 10

Turning her head away from the community centre entrance swiftly, DI Alice Mann rushed along the path to where her car was parked on a yellow, zig-zagged line. Despite having investigated dozens of violent deaths through her work, nothing filled her with more dread these days than the nursery drop-off.

Charlie was at an age when he knew precisely where he was going when she or Fergus strapped him into his car seat and set off in the direction of the Cragganhall Community Centre where the nursery was housed. He had a growing vocabulary and this now included the plaintive cry, "Don't want to go, Mummy!" The phrase had become an all-too familiar accompaniment to the short drive.

Alice knew her son enjoyed his time there, once he'd settled in and had even made a few little pals, but the moment she left him bawling in the arms of one of the assistants each morning never got any easier to bear.

Fergus had to constantly reassure her it was the right thing to do. She had a high-flying career that Charlie would be greatly proud of one day. Fergus himself was a busy defence advocate who could hardly spare much time from his own working day.

Guiltily, Alice pulled out into the thick, slow line of traffic and put all thoughts of her son firmly to the back of her mind. She was going to interview Macy McAdams, the spokesperson for Earth's Saviours that morning, along with Sharon Moffett. They'd agreed to meet at the group's headquarters near the Cathedral. Alice wasn't required to go into the office first, so she'd have time to drop Charlie off. This type of special treatment made Alice deeply uncomfortable. But she didn't have any other choice.

The city centre was eerily free of traffic. Alice knew the uniforms were keeping out all but official vehicles but it still felt odd. She found a space on Castle Street with ease. Sharon was already outside the building waiting for her.

"They've got an office on the fourth floor," the DS explained as Alice approached. "They're expecting us."

The DI stared up at the tall stone façade. "I suppose I expected their headquarters to be somewhere more *earthy*."

Sharon smiled. "Like an old bothy on a hillside, you mean?"

"Something like that." Alice led the way inside. The first floor housed an insurance broker, the second an accountancy firm and the third a solicitors' office. The fourth floor landing appeared little different to the others, except the plaque by the door looked handmade and was embossed with a curled dragon.

Sharon knocked.

A young, thin man in a cheesecloth shirt answered. "Can I help you?" His eyes were almond-shaped like a snake.

"We've got an appointment with Ms McAdams." Alice showed him her ID.

The man didn't try to hide his disgust. "Follow me," he grunted.

The third floor of the building had clearly never been used as offices like the first three. It was more like a vast attic storeroom. Steel supports reached up to the apex of the roof and dust hung thick in the air around them. Daylight was provided by a couple of skylights in the roof itself. There were no desks, but dozens of people were seated in groups across the dirty floorboards, some deep in discussion, others constructing the huge banners they'd seen at the demo the previous day.

Amongst one of the groups, Macy McAdams was sitting cross-legged, smoking a roll-up cigarette. Her braids were twisted on top of her head and she wore a wide, billowing, cotton dress and heavy boots. Alice wanted to inform her that smoking was not permitted in the workplace, but she wasn't entirely sure this was a workplace and knew they'd need the woman's cooperation. She bit her tongue.

"Ms McAdams, we met the other day at the protest. I'm DI Alice Mann and this is DS Moffett."

The woman stood, blowing smoke into the air. "Yes, I remember. How can I help you? I'm not going to give away all our secrets. I told you that."

"If we could talk privately, that would be better. It's a delicate matter."

Macy McAdams looked amused. "There's a meditation space under the eaves. We can go there."

The space she was referring to was a corner of the loft which had been swept clean and scattered with jute rugs and cushions. Alice spied a couple of low stools with relief and dragged them over for her and Sharon.

McAdams settled in the centre of one of the large cushions, covered with a woven kilim fabric. "The man who owns this building is sympathetic to our cause. He lets us use the top floor rent free. It has been very useful for us with the conference taking place in the city."

"Yes, I can see it would. But we are here about something else."

McAdams tipped her head curiously.

"We are investigating a death which occurred in suspicious circumstances on the day after we saw you at the wharf."

"A murder?" McAdams looked genuinely shocked.

"I'm afraid so. With the conference ongoing, we are hoping to keep the details out of the press for as long as possible, so your discretion would be appreciated." Alice wondered how far they could trust this woman, whose aim was to disrupt their plans in order to get her message across. But the woman's expression was troubled rather than calculating.

"I've been following all the news bulletins about the conference and I haven't heard a single word about a *murder*?"

"We're trying to keep the story out of the press. I believe it's in everyone's interest for this conference to continue. You wish to push for greater reforms, but without this platform, there would be no reforms at all. We don't believe the death has any direct bearing on the climate conference itself, so it should be able to continue, but that depends on us dealing with this investigation swiftly and without media involvement."

McAdams looked thoughtful. "I understand. Someone is dead, but if the planet continues to deteriorate, thousands will die of famines and floods. We have a greater cause to protect."

"Exactly," Sharon chipped in. "There were certain details about the way in which the victim died, which have led us here."

McAdams shook her head. "I don't understand."

"The symbol of the cross that you were using in your demonstration. Do you make them yourselves?" Sharon glanced about the room, where all sorts of handicrafts were being performed; from banner writing to weaving wicker baskets.

"No, we don't as a rule. We have a very active group in the Argyll Forest. They volunteer for Woodland Scotland and are able to use offcuts of wood to make the crosses for us. There are oak, birch and even some ash and alder trees there. They use whatever they can. They even provide the willow for us to produce our baskets: we use them to deliver our leaflets and also sell them at fairs to raise money for the cause."

"Could you provide us with the contact details for this group?"

"Hang on, why are you so interested in our crosses? What on earth can they have to do with your murder investigation?"

Alice took a deep breath. "A wooden cross, very similar to the ones you take on marches was found at the scene of the suspicious death."

McAdams jumped to her feet. "What!? Are you here because you think my group has been involved in a murder!?"

Alice glanced around nervously, hoping the woman's words hadn't travelled. "At this time, we are simply investigating every angle. The presence of a handmade cross at the scene which was almost identical to the ones you carry is too much of a coincidence to ignore."

McAdams shook her head wildly. "Where was this person killed anyway? *How* were they killed?" Realisation seemed to dawn on the woman and she dropped heavily back onto the cushion, having the presence of mind to lower her voice again. "Holy shit. The cross was the bloody *murder weapon*, wasn't it?"

The detectives said nothing.

McAdams began chewing on nails already halfway to the quick. "Okay. This is bad. When the press get hold of it, they'll have a field day. Most of the broadsheets hate us anyway; think we're all over-privileged grungies who have dropped out of life. If they can suggest Earth's Saviours are connected to a *murder*, all our hard work to change public opinion will be undone."

Alice leant forward. “We have no desire to go public with this information. Yet. If you cooperate with us fully, we may be able to tie up our investigation without the circus of media speculation.”

McAdams nodded distractedly. “Of course. I’ll cooperate as much as I can. But once you start asking more questions, within this group and beyond, we may not be able to keep this quiet for long.”

Alice sighed, she was relieved to have the group leader’s cooperation, but also knew she was absolutely right.

Chapter 11

Dermot glanced around at the bustling department. He'd asked the DCI to call a meeting. The results of the *post-mortem* were back. The DI was also glad to see his colleagues had returned from questioning their witnesses. He glanced at the clock and raised his hand. A hush fell over the assembled officers, who quietly turned their chairs in the direction of the smartboard. DCI Bevan emerged from her office to join them.

"Okay folks, I've got the results back from Dr Neill's office." Dermot summoned up a document on the screen. "I've had a skim through the findings and I'll try to give you the headlines. Stomach contents showed that Quentin Lester had eaten breakfast approximately three hours before his death, which tallies with what we already know. He'd made the most of the complimentary buffet by putting away a full English by all accounts. The deceased was moderately overweight and an examination of his organs indicated early signs of liver disease and significant furring of his coronary arteries. There was no evidence of recent sexual activity or of any struggle between perpetrator and victim."

"So he wasn't in the best of health, then?" Dani interrupted.

"No, he wasn't," Dermot crinkled his brow. "Which explains the pathologist's conclusion on cause of death." He flicked back to one of the crime scene photos, which showed Lester on the bed, the cross embedded in his chest through the ripped fabric of his shirt, a few pathetic wisps of curly white hair surrounding the wooden protuberance. "The cross, which had been roughly sharpened to a point at the end which penetrated the body, actually entered the chest cavity between the left lung and the heart. It had avoided any major arteries and this was the reason for there being so little blood at the scene."

Alice raised her hand. "Then why did it kill him?"

"Good question," Dermot continued. "The answer is that it didn't."

A few puzzled glances were exchanged amongst the officers gathered.

"If medical assistance had arrived in time and the weapon remained in place, surgery could certainly have saved him from the stab wound. However, Dr Neill suggests that Lester's arteries were dangerously clogged before he was attacked in that hotel room. The stabbing, or even the stress of the attack, brought on a massive myocardial infarction. It was this that killed him in a matter of minutes."

"Does this mean it wasn't actually murder?" Tyler Sullivan was genuinely confused. This was his first case in major crime.

Dani stepped forward. "Although I've not seen a case quite like this one before, I have worked on murders where a heart attack brought on by a violent act has been the cause of death. We still treat this as murder. The defence lawyers will use the information to try and reduce the sentence, of course, when the case comes to trial with a defendant. But we treat the investigation just the same." She turned to Dermot. "Had Lester been aware of his cardiovascular disease? Do his records show he was on any medication?"

Dermot shook his head. "Lester's records indicate he hardly ever visited a doctor. He'd been abroad for several years, so we don't know what kind of treatment he'd sought there, but Dr Neill said his heart condition had been untreated for at least five years or more."

Dan Clifton got to his feet. “We know that Lester worked for a charity in Dodoma until four years ago when he returned to the UK. Tyler and I are still investigating that lead, Ma’am.”

“Good, we need that information as soon as possible. Perhaps he made some enemies out there?”

Dermot switched the screen back to the forensic report. “What strikes me most about the cause of death, is that although our perpetrator had a sharpened weapon to use at close range, they still didn’t manage to pierce the heart or the lung.”

Alice narrowed her eyes. “So despite the careful dressing of the scene; with the weird academic gown and handmade cross, they didn’t really know what they were doing when it came to killing a man.”

Sharon piped up, “so we aren’t talking about a professional hit. This person was an amateur. Maybe it *was* some kind of sexual game gone wrong? The victim was on a promise of dress-up sex and a bit of S and M, but the role play got out of hand?”

Dermot shook his head. “The evidence is contradictory. There were no prints on the weapon or in the room other than Lester’s and the cleaning staff. The attacker was very careful about that. If they were just in that room for a kinky sexual encounter, they wouldn’t have taken such forensic care. I think the staging took place after death. Yet they botched the killing itself. His phone records don’t show any calls in the days leading up to his death, so if he called a girlfriend or a prostitute to meet him that day at the hotel, it didn’t happen on his home phone, or the hotel telephone. There was a call to his mobile, which he usually barely made use of, from a number we are currently tracing, at just before 12pm. It lasted a couple of minutes. This was the first time this number had appeared on his records, which were brief as it was. It could’ve been a sales call even. The technical officers are still going through his laptop and digital footprint. His car, a two year old Toyota Yaris, was still in its space in the SEC underground carpark. It was kept clean and neat, with only Lester's DNA present on the interior. He didn't call or message people much on the phone we have and his emails were purely relating to business. He 'kept himself to himself' in every sense of the phrase."

Dani breathed deeply. "He sounds like he was someone trying to live a simple life, without the complications of human relationships. It's easy enough to learn how to cover your tracks forensically; and even to lure a middle-aged, lonely man to a hotel room at lunchtime without leaving a trace; perhaps she or he approached him on the way between the SEC and the hotel? But unless you're a psychopath or a professional, it isn't so easy to kill a man in cold blood when they're looking you in the eye, or even pleading for mercy."

"So we're looking for someone who has never killed before?" Sharon made eye contact with her boss.

"I believe that is correct. How about the CCTV from the hotel, Dermot?"

"One of the security team at the SEC has been examining the recordings. He's due to get back to me today."

"Can you call him and speed that up. I want to get our first glimpse of the killer." Dani turned to Alice. "What about the murder weapon? Do you think it came from the Earth's Saviours organisation?"

"The weapon had been wiped completely clean of prints, as Dermot said, but the design is incredibly similar to those used by the eco-group. Ms McAdams has agreed to cooperate with us. She doesn't want her group implicated in a murder. She's given us the address of the place where the crosses are made for them, up in the Argyll Forest. If I took detailed photos of our weapon and showed it to the people who actually make them, we might be able to confirm a match?"

Dani sighed. "Okay, take Sharon with you and make the trip. Let's hope it's not a blind alley. It's very possible that cross was simply made in someone's garage and has no connection to Earth's Saviours at all."

Dan Clifton piped up. "From what Lester's boss told us at his office in Stirling, he was a completely nondescript type of character; with few friends and no family currently living with him, or even visiting. His house was neat and tidy and his personal effects haven't thrown up anything of interest. Yet his murder was bizarre and deeply symbolic in the choice of staging and weapon. I think Alice and Sharon are right, there's got to be a greater significance to the cross."

Dani turned to her junior officer. "With a murder so bizarre, unless we're talking about a case of mistaken identity, which is pretty much impossible, as Lester would have been wearing an ID lanyard when he met his killer, there had to be something more about this man. His life in the last four years in Scotland had been entirely bland. But what was he up to before that time? It had to be so bad he was targeted for some kind of ritual murder. It's up to you and DC Sullivan to find that out. Dig into his time in Africa and what he'd been up to before that. Where are his first wife and kids and why did he have no contact with them? This was a man trying to live below the radar. I want to know why."

Dermot stepped forward with determination in his gait. "You heard the boss. Now, let's get to work."

Chapter 12

Rain was battering the roof of Alice's hatchback, the stream of water being only briefly interrupted by the swish of the windscreen wipers. Muttering thanks to some nameless power, she pulled into a space just feet from the front gate of their ground floor flat.

Alice turned off the engine and glanced into the back. Charlie was secured into his car seat, his face red with pent-up frustration, his feet in solid boots drumming against the seat in front. Alice knew her son was tired and probably hungry after his day at nursery, they'd also not been able to take the little ones out into the playground because of the weather. She sensed a meltdown was imminent.

"It's a bit wet out there, sweetie. Mum's just going to open the front door and then come back for you. So you don't get too wet."

Charlie appeared to understand this statement and its implications entirely as his chocolate brown eyes widened to their full extent and tears pooled at their edges.

Alice pulled up her hood and wrenched open the car door. The downpour showed no sign of letting up. She had to jump over an already deep puddle to reach the pavement. She pulled open Charlie's door so that he could watch her from his seat and know she hadn't abandoned him.

It took her about a minute and a half to dash down the path and unlock the front door. When she turned back towards the road, a dark figure was leaning into the rear of the car, where she'd left the door open, where Charlie was strapped in his seat. It was all Alice could do not to let out a scream.

She sprinted through the gate, “What’s going on?” Alice demanded.

The figure righted itself. It was a woman, not much younger than Alice. She had a black raincoat on and her face was neatly made-up. “I’m really sorry, you must be Mum. I was walking past and I heard a child crying, I just looked into the car to check he was okay. We were having a little chat. He’s fine now.”

Alice looked past the woman at her son. Wet streaks were visible down his podgy cheeks, but he was no longer crying. He was watching the stranger with rapt interest. “I was just opening the front door so he wouldn’t get too wet when I carried him in. I was only a couple of minutes.” Alice wondered why she felt so defensive.

The woman cracked a friendly smile. “Oh, not to worry. I kept an eye on him for you.”

“Well, I’d better get him inside now, thanks.”

The woman stepped back and clip-clopped away on low but stylish heels. Alice instinctively unclipped Charlie from his seat and held him to her breast, not caring now about the rain and wondering what on earth had just happened.

*

Fergus was back in time to bath Charlie and put him to bed. As the lawyer re-entered the living room, which stretched from the front to the rear of the flat, he found Alice slumped on the sofa, a bottle of wine and two glasses on the coffee table in front of her.

“Tough day?” He raised an eyebrow and poured a glass of red for them both.

“It was busy. This murder investigation is far from straightforward. It’s incredibly rare for a murderer to stage the crime scene in such a specific way. Sharon and I are looking into the origin of the murder weapon." She took a glug of wine and grimaced. "We're going to have to drive up to the Argyll Forest tomorrow, that's where the Earth's Saviours crosses are made."

Fergus placed an arm around her shoulders. "My case has finished. I can drop Charlie off and pick him up tomorrow. That's fine."

Alice kissed his cheek. "Thanks, but I'll need you to be vigilant when you bring him back home."

Fergus frowned. "Aren't I always?"

"Of course." Alice shuffled up in her seat, took a breath and explained about the incident with the strange woman at the car that afternoon.

Fergus sipped his wine. "It seems like she was harmless enough in the end. But I will look out for her tomorrow, in case she's hanging around. Neither of us are amateurs, we know what people are capable of."

Alice shuddered and leaned into his chest. "Do you really think she may have taken Charlie, if I hadn't come back?"

"It's hard to say. Odds are, she heard a toddler crying and wanted to help. Unfortunately, we tend to get involved in the very rare cases when someone decides to do more than that. It makes us overly suspicious."

"I gave her an opportunity."

"There are always opportunities. We will have to get used to that as Charlie gets older. Most people are good and decent and wish children no harm." He gave her a squeeze.

"I didn't sense she wanted to harm Charlie, if I'm honest. It felt more like she was shaming me, for leaving him alone for a second."

"Whereas there are *plenty* of people out there who want to shame us for our parenting."

Alice smiled. That was certainly true. She resolved to forget about the woman at the car. Charlie hadn't been bothered by the incident at all. Instead, she decided to pick her partner's legal brain. "We got the *PM* results back today. It seems the victim didn't die from his stab injury at all, despite how horrendous it looked. The attack brought on a massive heart attack. He'd suffered from heart disease for years. Have you come across a case like that before? When a murder victim actually died of natural causes?"

Fergus nodded, draining his glass. "Actually, I have. But it's always been related to domestic violence cases, or brawls. In one incident, a man had pushed his wife down the stairs in their home. She was knocked unconscious and suffered a heart attack, dying within minutes. There was fresh bruising on her upper arms consistent with a tight grip."

"Did you defend the husband?"

"Yes, he got ten years for manslaughter. The prosecution couldn't prove any previous longstanding abuse."

Alice put down her glass on the table and turned to face him. "So the cause of death *did* make a difference to the charge and sentencing?"

"In this case, it did. But I could argue that a shove down the stairs in anger didn't necessarily entail the intent to kill. It was most likely an argument; emotions were heated. Because of the coronary, there was no evidence the fall would have killed her on its own or that she hadn't tripped at the top of the stairs during the altercation. But in your case, there was clear premeditation. The killer brought a specially made weapon; items to dress the scene. There's no way a jury would imagine that a stab to the chest with a sharpened stake wouldn't be intended to cause death. Juries aren't stupid."

"Yeah, I see what you mean. The staging was almost comical; the black robe and sharpened cross. It was like a satanic ritual maybe. But then the murderer botched the stabbing itself, missing the vital organs."

"Perhaps this is their first kill."

Alice considered this idea, knowing Sharon felt the same. "DCS Douglas has allowed us to use an analyst to cross-reference our scene with other cases to see if there have been any murders in the UK with a similar MO. Because the First Minister wants the climate conference to go ahead without mishap, we've been given a decent budget to solve this case quickly."

"Your analyst should look at assaults as well as murders. This could be a perpetrator who has escalated their crimes. Maybe looking at any crime scene including dress-up and ritual would be worthwhile."

"I will inform her." She snuggled back into his chest, glad she had a partner it was possible to share these things with. She suspected most young men would be repelled by such a discussion over their cosy evening drink.

Chapter 13

A low-level buzz of activity filled the floor of the department, like honey bees in a flower meadow on a sunny day. Dan Clifton had moved Tyler Sullivan to join him at his workstation. They'd both had their heads lowered over their desks for most of the morning.

Dan tossed a biro onto a pile of papers and stretched his arms above his head. "Fancy a coffee?" He called over to his colleague.

Tyler raised his head, looking a little bemused. "I don't drink coffee, or tea. I kinda think of it as the stuff my parents would have."

Dan's face crinkled into a smile. He used to be the young, trendy member of the department. The world was changing fast. "What *do* you drink then?"

Tyler rubbed his smooth chin. "If I'm in a café I'll usually order one of those smoothie things. Anything with fruit and ice."

"Well, I don't think the drinks tray can stretch to that. But I could get you a can of something from the machine?"

"Yeah, sure, that'd be great. Thanks."

Dan fished in his pocket for some small change. He parted with a couple of fifties at the vending machine in exchange for a bottle of lemonade claiming to contain real fruit. He figured that would do. He carried it back to the trestle table in the corner of the department housing a kettle and an assortment of chipped mugs. He didn't care what the young folk did these days, he needed a caffeine fix. He didn't mind this sort of research task either, but he sensed Tyler was itching to get back out into the field.

Dan placed the bottle next to Tyler's computer

and sipped from his own cup as he sat back down. "Found anything of interest?"

Tyler looked up. He twisted the lid of the bottle and glugged from it thirstily. "Cheers, mate. I've had some luck tracking down the identity of Lester's ex-wife." He glanced down at his notepad. "They got married in 1988 in a registry office in Dornoch. The divorce was finalised in 2003. Her name is Fiona. But that's as far as I've got. No current address yet. She may have remarried."

"Dornoch? That's a lot further north than Stirling."

"Aye, the children were both born at Raigmore Hospital in Inverness in the early nineties, so they must have lived around that area for a while. It certainly fits with the employment record Mrs Meakin gave us. He studied at the University of the Highlands between 1982 and '85. Then, he worked for a housing charity in Inverness for many years. No convictions during that time, not even a parking ticket that I can find."

"Any luck tracking down the children? They really need to be informed of their father's death as next of kin. But neither has come forward to report him missing, even. They must have been estranged. I found no correspondence between them in his personal effects. Not even a birthday card."

"The son was named Ian. He'd be 29 years old now. The daughter was Elinor and she'd be 32. She could have got married, maybe? Changed her name?"

Dan nodded. "You'll have to check the databases. If neither of them have any criminal convictions then they must have driving licences."

"Unless they moved abroad?"

"We'll cross that bridge if we come to it."

"Speaking of living abroad, have you found out

much about Lester's time in Africa?"

Dan sighed. "He stopped paying tax in the UK at the start of 2012. According to the references he gave Mrs Meakin, he'd worked at a small charity operating out of Dodoma, Tanzania. They were set up by a man called Simon Clarke and raised money to build schools and improve the infrastructure of villages in the southern region of Masasi. According to his CV, Lester was a fundraiser for the charity, alongside selecting projects for them to take on. He left the post in 2018."

"So, he spent six years in Africa." Tyler gulped more of his drink. "DCI Bevan seemed particularly interested in this period of Lester's life. Can we find out any more about the life he led out there? I can't quite see how it would connect to his bizarre murder, ten years later, at the SEC in Glasgow, though."

"No, but I can see why Bevan is interested. It's an unusual aspect of the victim's background. Something that sets him apart from the ordinary." Dan glanced at his watch. "Dodoma are three hours ahead of us. I'm going to try ringing Clarke's office now. If he takes a lunchbreak, he should be back at his desk."

Tyler drained the bottle dry and tossed it into a nearby bin. "Good idea. I need to find out some more about Lester's kids. Let's just hope they aren't on the other side of the world too."

*

The lift doors opened. A tall, blond-haired woman in her mid-thirties stepped onto the floor of the serious crime division. A few officers briefly turned their heads, interested in seeing a new face.

Dermot got up from his desk and approached her. "Klara Laska? I'm DI Muir, the DCS asked me to liaise with you on the case details."

The woman nodded her head and followed Dermot to a desk he had temporarily cleared. She took a seat and began unpacking a laptop and files. "I have already looked through the reports you sent me. I've noted the key characteristics of the murder scene. What type of parameters would you like me to apply to my search?"

Dermot creased his forehead. "To be honest, I've never worked with an analyst before. You may have to guide me on this."

Klara smiled. "Not all cases have the budget to use my services. I lecture in Criminal Studies at the university. I have a BSC in psychology and a MSC in digital forensics. I work on a freelance basis for Police Scotland, although I have travelled to England and Ireland to assist in high-profile cases there too."

"We're very lucky to have you," Dermot said with feeling. He scratched his head of thick hair. "The way that Quentin Lester's body had been staged and the choice of murder weapon struck us as very unusual. We want to know if there have been any other cases where similar staging was evident."

Klara nodded thoughtfully. "The staging of a crime scene is incredibly rare in the UK. It tells us a great deal about the mindset of the killer and their driving motives."

Dermot took the chair opposite. "We thought the set-up might be sexual. He was in his hotel room at lunchtime, his clothing below the waist had been removed down to his socks. Yet there was no sign of recent sexual activity on the body."

Klara summoned up the scene photographs on her laptop. She pointed at the screen. "Do you see the way the academic robe has been placed around the man's shoulders?"

Dermot peered closely.

"There is more of the gown on the man's left side

than the right. It seems as if the material has been tugged under his body on this right side. You can see it is twisted slightly under the armpit, caught on the shirt sleeve?"

Dermot nodded. "You think it was placed on the body after death?"

"Yes, I do. The body was heavy, so the killer couldn't pull the gown out evenly on both sides. They were under time pressure, so had to leave it as it was and flee the hotel. My initial guess is that he undressed himself down below, but after death, the gown was added."

"Yes, I can see that makes sense. The windows in the room only opened a couple of inches. The killer had to make their escape through the body of the hotel, so they were under a pressure of time to make their getaway. The staging must have taken place in a hurry. I'm expecting the CCTV recordings from the building any time now."

"Good. Hopefully you will get an image of your killer. In the meantime, I would suggest I begin my analysis of crime scene data going back ten years within the UK? If we don't get any matches, we can expand the parameters, yes?"

Dermot readily agreed. He was prepared to take the lead from this seemingly professional and extremely capable woman.

Chapter 14

It was a clear but cold day on the Cowal Peninsula. Alice drove along the banks of Loch Fyne, where the sun was high in the sky over the navy blue surface of the deep water. Her Sat Nav abruptly instructed her to turn down a track which took them through a dense forest of Silver Birch trees and saplings.

Sharon peered into the tightly packed lines of trees, where the light of the early November sun was almost extinguished. "I prefer mountains and water myself," she commented idly.

"You get both here on the peninsula. We had a family holiday in Strachur once." Alice swung the car into a space beside a single-storey building positioned at the centre of a clearing. The 'Woodland Scotland' sign took pride of place by the entrance, itself having been whittled from an impressive lump of oak.

Alice knocked hard on the door. Eventually, a man in his late forties, with thinning hair and wearing a green jumper with an acorn motif, opened up. She showed him her ID. "I called ahead and spoke with a Mr McCleary?"

He nodded and stood back to allow them to enter. "That's me. Todd McCleary. We've just closed to the public for the winter season, so there aren't many staff here."

The building housed an information centre with boards depicting the types of trees and foliage found in the forest and models of the landscaping and conservation projects the organisation had been carrying out. McCleary led them to an office down a narrow corridor.

"I've just made a pot of coffee. Would you like one?"

Sharon opened her mouth to accept but Alice got in first. "No thanks. This shouldn't take long."

The man shrugged, gesturing to a pair of seats in front of an untidy desk. "What can I do for you?"

"I believe there are a number of volunteers who work in the forest throughout the year?"

He nodded, waiting for the DI to continue.

"We have been informed that you allow some of your volunteers to take unwanted offcuts of wood, which they then take away from the forest for their own uses?"

McCleary frowned. "Yes, we have a team of trained volunteers. They do all kinds of jobs; from running the tearoom to helping clear the dead and diseased trees. We couldn't function without them. A group of young guys assist with the clearing and felling. Most of the wood is sold to the local sawmill, but the offcuts are certainly up for grabs. But you're wrong in one respect."

Alice raised an eyebrow. "What is that?"

"The wood doesn't leave the forest, well, not until it's been transformed into something else." He gestured towards the dense rows of silvery trunks just outside the tiny office window. "The woodworking guys have a cabin in the woods themselves, they rent it from us at a small rate but have modified it for their purposes. They have their own woodworking tools and machinery. They produce all kinds of hand turned goods, which then sell in local craft shops. The boys are busy all year round." He broke into a friendly smile. "We even sell some items here in the shop. You won't find a more sustainable souvenir of the forest than an item honed right here from the trees themselves. We only cut timber that has become diseased or growths which are preventing the thriving of other flora and fauna. We are at the cutting edge of forest management. If you pardon the pun."

The officers got to their feet, they didn't have time for the manager's sales pitch, or his bad jokes. "And where exactly might we find this cabin?" Alice asked determinedly.

Chapter 15

Sharon clutched the map and scanned the path ahead of them. The atmosphere was damp and chilly. "It's getting darker the further we go into the forest." She shivered.

"I'm not sure I'd want to spend all my time in here. You'd barely see the sun."

"And we see little enough of that in Scotland as it is."

Alice chuckled. "There! Just off to the right. I can see a chimney giving off smoke."

"Aye I see it too. At least it might be warm in this hut."

They only needed to take a few more steps before the hut and its occupants became clearly visible. A fire was burning in a wire brazier at the centre of a man-made clearing. Three men were busy at work in front of a small wooden hut with a pointed roof, but it looked as though much of their activities took place outside. A canvas canopy, secured between the tall branches of a couple of oaks protected their equipment from the elements and the fire appeared to be providing light and heat.

Alice approached carefully with her warrant card held aloft. One of the men was operating some kind of lathe. She didn't want to cause a nasty accident by taking them by surprise.

The man looked up, his sandy-blond hair drooping over his forehead and turned off his machine. "Hi, can we help you at all?"

"I'm DI Alice Mann and this is DS Moffett from Police Scotland. May we have a few words?"

The man lifted off his ear protectors. The other two stopped what they were doing and exchanged puzzled glances. “Sure. Come and take a seat by the fire.”

A couple of large logs had been placed on their sides and smooth seats hollowed out of the bark. Sharon found it surprisingly comfortable.

The man who had spoken remained standing. “I’m Justin and this is Harry and Jake. I’m not sure how we can be of any assistance to you?”

Alice opened her bag and brought out a file of photographs in plastic cases. The images showed the murder weapon used against Quentin Lester; cleaned after the forensic tests and positioned at various angles. “We were informed by Macy McAdams, leader of the Earth’s Saviours organisation, that you make wooden crosses for use at their demonstrations.” She handed him the photos. “I wondered if you recognised this one?”

Justin took the file of pictures. “We are all sympathetic to the Earth’s Saviours’ cause, and every other climate change activist group operating in Scotland.” He gestured to their surroundings. “We see first-hand the impact of human greed on the environment. Deforestation around the world is killing our planet.”

Alice didn’t really want the political polemic. “Yes, I can see how your interests would tally with theirs. Is it true you make the crosses for them? They needed a great number for the COP26 conference?”

Justin glanced nervously about him. “Yeah, it is true. Harry’s sister goes on every one of their marches. He takes them down to Glasgow to give to her. But I haven’t mentioned it to Mr McCleary. He’s happy to provide us with wood for making stools and garden decorations, but if he thought we were using it for something *political,* I reckon his bosses wouldn’t be happy. They say all the right stuff about stopping climate change, but it's all talk of the corporate bullshit variety, you know?"

Alice suspected he was right. "We aren't interested in where Earth's Saviours get their props from. Our interest is just in that cross there. If you could give me some information about it, there's no need for me to mention anything to Mr McCleary."

He looked relieved, staring more closely at the pictures. "Hey, Harry, come over a minute, will you?"

Another of the young men, aged also in his late twenties, stopped chiselling an impressive wooden sculpture of an owl and stepped towards them. He examined the pictures his friend handed him. "What's this?"

Sharon piped up. "It's a cross that was used in a crime. We believe it is very similar to the types of cross you've been making for Earth's Saviours."

Harry glanced nervously at the other man.

"It's ok," Justin replied. "They aren't interested in that. Just this particular cross."

Harry scrunched up his rugged features. "I'd say the wood is ash. We've been clearing a lot of ash trees here in recent years, due to the spread of Dieback. It's a very strong material and looks lovely if it's properly sanded and oiled." He ran his hand through messy, knotted curls. "But this is badly made. The screws have been put in at an angle and the wood is very rough at the end. It would give anyone handling it some nasty splinters. It's also been sharpened at the other end, more like a stake to put in the ground. I don't do them like that."

"So, you didn't make this?" Sharon asked bluntly.

Harry eyed her with surprise. "No way. I'd never give my sister crosses like this. I make them as a symbol of the spiritual power of nature, but also as a celebration of the beauty that can be made from natural products." He looked affronted.

Alice felt her heart sink. She looked over at the stunning owl he was carving and knew this was true. "Okay, well, thanks for your time." They got to their feet. "Are you the only volunteers here who use the offcuts from the tree clearing?"

"We are the only ones who asked for permission and for the use of this hut. Our products are sold in the craft shop by the entrance, it suits us and Woodland Scotland. But I couldn't say for certain that other volunteers aren't pocketing the scraps." Justin shrugged his shoulders.

Alice took back the file of pictures and stuffed it in her bag, slinging it in frustration over her shoulder. She and Sharon fell into step beside one another, heading back in the direction of the entrance.

"We could always get a list of all the volunteers from Todd McCleary?" Sharon offered cheerily.

"Yeah, we will do that," Alice said resignedly. But she felt the weight of disappointment pressing on her chest as they tramped back through the forest. Tears were even prickling her tired eyes. The trip had taken up an entire day with very little to show for it and she'd miss Charlie's bedtime too. They had a long journey home.

As if sensing her colleague's loss of heart, Sharon nudged Alice's arm. "Hey, I reckon we got some good information there. When I was researching Earth's Saviours before the conference, I saw a lot of photos of those crosses being used in protests. No matter what that Harry said, a lot of them were pretty roughly made, like our murder weapon. I reckon these lads in the forest aren't the only ones making crosses for Macy McAdams and her group, whether she's aware of it or not."

Alice glanced at Sharon, her downturned mouth creeping up into a smile. “I think you might very well be right.”

Chapter 16

The images themselves were crisp and sharp, but the foyer and corridors were so dingy and filled with shadows that it made identifying anyone shown in them a difficult task.

Dermot squinted again at the screen on his laptop where the screenshots were enlarged to their maximum. He rolled back his chair and leant out onto the office floor, gripping the door frame. He spotted Dan Clifton carrying a mug of coffee to his desk. "Hey, Dan! Could you come and help me with something?"

The younger detective put down his drink and strode towards the office. "Sure, what can I do?"

Dermot twisted around his laptop and pointed at the screen. "I've just received the CCTV footage of the day Lester was murdered from the security team at the SEC."

Dan nodded, examining the image closely.

"The images recorded will really help us to create a timeline of Lester's movements that day. He went to breakfast at the hotel alone, leaving in time to sign into the conference centre at 9am. Cameras caught him exiting a lecture theatre at 12pm, but he didn't go to lunch at the canteen, instead he exited the building at a few minutes past. Not long after he received a two minute phone call from a pay-as-you-go number which is now disconnected."

"Okay, so what about the hotel? Does anyone re-enter with him?"

Dermot nodded. "Yes, this is the best image I could find. Lester is seen entering the hotel reception at 12.33pm. Look at the figure just behind him."

Dan looked closely. "They're wearing a dark coat, probably black, with a hood. I'd say a similar height to Lester but a slimmer build. To be honest, I can't even tell if it's a man or a woman."

Dermot sighed heavily, leaning back in the swivel chair. "Neither can I. We have thirty minutes unaccounted for. It barely takes five minutes to walk from the conference centre to the hotel."

"Perhaps he was meeting this person during that time, talking down by the river, maybe?"

"Yes, sure. But was it pre-arranged, or spur of the moment?"

"They certainly hadn't been communicating prior to that day via Lester's mobile phone or email," Dan offered.

"I've looked through all of the footage. This is the clearest image we have of the person we assume to be our killer. They exited the hotel at 1.25pm. But at this point, we only see them from behind and the hood is up again."

Dan whistled. "They certainly cut it fine. The security teams noticed Lester was missing from his meeting at ten past one and you'd decided to check out his hotel maybe fifteen minutes later. You can't have missed the perp by very long."

Dermot had worked this out for himself. "The killer targeted Lester whilst he was attending the most high-profile and tightly monitored conference Scotland has ever hosted. You and Sullivan suggested he lived a lonely and simple existence in Stirling, so why not target him there? He lived alone, had well established habits?"

"What does DCI Bevan think?"

"She's in a meeting with the DCS right now, but I'll be showing her these the minute she returns."

"I spoke with the man who employed Lester in Dodoma from 2012 until 2018, Simon Clarke. He still works out in Tanzania. According to him, Lester was a quiet man who worked hard and seemed dedicated to the charity's aims. He provided him with a good reference when he decided to return to the UK."

Dermot ran a hand through his thick fringe. "What was it that made this ordinary-seeming man a target? We don't seem to be getting any closer to finding that out."

"Tyler and I will keep digging into the man's past. We've also still got to hear from Alice and Sharon about their trip to Argyll Forest. I bet they've found out something really important for us."

Dermot wished he shared his colleague's optimism. He knew Sharon well. If they'd had a breakthrough in their quest to find the source of the murder weapon, he would have heard about it by now.

Chapter 17

James was working late and Dani had decided to cook herself a simple meal at their Scotstounhill flat. She was tidying away and filling the dishwasher with a single pot and plate when the doorbell sounded.

Dani padded down the corridor to see a familiar figure through the frosted glass panel of the front door. She pulled it open.

DS Andy Calder stood on the step, still dressed in his high-vis jacket. "Evening, Ma'am. I was patrolling this area and thought I'd drop in. If that's okay? I'm off duty now."

"Of course, come in and have a drink, get that damp gear off and warm up."

Andy shook off the jacket gratefully and unzipped his Kevlar vest, allowing them to drop to the floor of the hallway in a damp heap. He rolled his shoulders with relief as he walked towards the kitchen.

"Coffee, or something stronger?" Dani asked.

"Is it possible to have both?" He lowered his weight onto a kitchen chair.

Dani chuckled. "How about coffee with a wee dash of whisky?"

"Perfect."

"How are your team getting on policing the conference? I hope you haven't felt side-lined, what with the rest of us busy on the murder enquiry?"

Andy rubbed his cold hands together vigorously, trying to get some blood flowing back into his numbed digits. "No, not at all. To be honest, I've enjoyed being back out on the streets. It reminds me of why I joined the force in the first place."

Dani placed a steaming cup on the table in front of him and took the seat opposite. "Has there been any trouble the last couple of days? DCS Douglas seems happy enough with how the conference is progressing?"

Andy sipped the coffee, feeling it warming him as it slid down. "Greta Thunberg addressed the conference yesterday morning, then she came out into George Square to speak to the protesters there. We tried to maintain a benign presence. There was no trouble, just the usual directing of people in and out. The press are the greatest pain in the arse of the lot, trying to get as close as possible to the lass. She looked like a wee waif up on that stage."

"And were the Earth's Saviours group there?" Dani sipped her own coffee, which was alcohol free.

"Oh aye, they're *everywhere*. You can see them a mile off with those daft crosses. When the crowds had cleared yesterday, the damn things were scattered across the entire square; bent and abandoned."

Dani grimaced. "Crosses just like our murder weapon are freely available in their hundreds all across the city."

"But it must have had a symbolic meaning for the killer, surely? This Lester guy is a delegate at the climate conference and the killer stakes him with a wooden cross used by the most prominent climate change protest group in Scotland?"

Dani cradled her cup. "If Lester had been a representative from an oil and gas company, who was lobbying for the continued reliance of the West on fossil fuels, I may have agreed with you. It would be obvious why a group opposed to climate change may want such a man dead, although still unlikely. But Quentin Lester worked for a *children's* charity. He was as dedicated to ending climate change for the benefit of the poorest children around the world as the Earth's Saviours are."

Andy supped in silence for a moment, his mind processing the details he'd been given. He placed his mug carefully on the table before replying. "Then maybe this murder isn't related to COP26 at all? The murderer has used all the whistles and bells of the conference to hide the fact this murder is one that's entirely personally motivated. It has nothing to do with climate change at all."

Dani nodded thoughtfully. "There was more to the staging of the murder scene than the cross alone. Our consultant analyst thinks the academic gown was placed onto Lester's body after death. We've tried to identify the gown. It wasn't connected to a particular academic institution but the type you'd buy in any dress-up shop; cheap and cheerful. We're still tracing suppliers but it could have come from somewhere online, or been in the killer's possession for years."

Andy crinkled his brow. "The body was dressed in a black robe and stabbed with a cross to the chest. It sounds like something from a Hammer House of Horrors movie."

Dani managed a thin smile. "Yes, there's certainly a potentially ritualistic, even satanic look to the murder scene. Our analyst is looking for murders that have had a similar MO in the past decade across the UK."

"Good idea. Because I get the feeling your killer *wants* you to get side-tracked by this climate activist angle. From what I've seen, most of them wouldn't slaughter an animal to eat even if they were dying of hunger. They aren't the murdering types, Ma'am. Pure and simple." He waggled his finger with emphasis, "now, the *journos* on the other hand, are a different matter entirely."

Dani finished her coffee and considered his words carefully; picking out the insight from the jaded humour, wishing she'd consulted Andy on these points a couple of days earlier.

Her old friend got slowly to his feet. “I’d better get back to Carol and Amy. It’s a hot bath and then bed for me. I’m on the early shift tomorrow.”

Dani pushed her chair back. “If you hang on a minute, I’ll give you a lift.”

Chapter 18

DC Tyler Sullivan remained inside the cabin of the boat. The waves were tipping them at forty-five degree angles and he was breathing hard to fight the nausea that was constricting his stomach.

Dan Clifton stuck his head through the hatch. "You're actually better off up on deck where you can see the horizon and get some air."

Tyler didn't even reply. He couldn't have shifted from his seat if he wanted to. Which he most certainly didn't.

Dan re-joined the skipper on deck. It was midday already. They had taken a small plane from Glasgow to mainland Orkney, but there was no airport where he and his colleague were heading. "How much further is it?" He called out, raising his voice to carry above the crashing waves of the turbulent sea.

"Another twenty minutes. North Dorga is a few miles south of Hoy. The big ferry from Aberdeen does stop there, which is more comfortable than a wee boat like ours, but it takes more than six hours."

"That's too long for us."

"What business do you have there?" The skipper eyed his passenger carefully. He knew the two younger men were police officers from Glasgow.

"We need to notify a next of kin about a sudden death."

"Could the local coppers not have done it? There's a small police station on North Dorga, none on South Dorga, though."

Dan gritted his teeth against a gust of salty spray that was whipped into his face as the boat took a nose dive into the sea. "This one needs to be face-to-face, unfortunately."

The skipper nodded his head solemnly. He'd

sailed boats around the Orkneys for several decades and considered himself to know something about the world. He assumed the presence of these young detectives, out on the unforgiving sea so far from home, meant the sudden death was very likely murder.

*

The weather had cleared by the time the boat reached the small harbour on the island of North Dorga. As Tyler stepped onto the stone pier his legs felt like jelly, but the gut-wrenching nausea had subsided.

Dan stepped confidently off the boat behind him. "Fancy some lunch before we head to the cop shop?"

Tyler grasped his stomach as a painful cramp made the stinging bile rise in his throat. "How can you even think about food after a journey like that?"

Dan couldn't resist a smile. "Once you get your sea-legs it doesn't seem quite so bad."

Tyler walked tentatively behind his colleague, shaking his head the whole way.

The police station on the island was located along the main street of the settlement they had landed in. The skipper had informed Dan it was called St Martin. There were just a half dozen stone buildings stretching along the small natural harbour, overlooking a shallow, pebbly crescent of beach. Beyond the buildings were a series of lush, undulating hills, but no mountains to speak of.

The officers at the station were expecting their arrival. Dan pushed through the heavy door of the single-storey structure and held it open for his partner, who seemed to have recovered his composure. The reception was open-plan. A large oak desk separated the entrance from a small office beyond, not even a Perspex screen offered any kind of delineation between the officers of the law and the general public.

The office was empty. Dan cleared his throat. “Afternoon!” His raised words seemed to evaporate into the stale air. Then, a door opened at the rear of the office and a middle-aged man with a pronounced widow’s peak and a tall, strong build emerged through it.

“You must be Sergeant Shewan? I’m DC Dan Clifton, from the Pitt Street HQ, and this is DC Tyler Sullivan.”

The man negotiated the small space to approach the solid wood desk and eyed his visitors carefully. “Eddie Shewan. Welcome to St Martin. There’s just myself and DC Harvey based here on the island. We’ve a population of just under a thousand. Tracy and I take on the job of detective, beat bobby, marriage guidance counsellor, childminder and whatever else service the locals might require.”

Dan noticed the man’s mouth turn up in a smile and recognised this as a favourite joke. “I don’t expect you get much serious crime out here?”

Eddie leant his powerful upper body on the counter-top. “Not like you’d understand it over in Glasgow. But often, the folk can be a law unto themselves out here. Some of the older families are used to doing their own thing. They don’t think that laws are quite as binding as they are back on the mainland.”

Dan nodded, he could understand that, being so remote from what he would consider civilisation. “We are here to interview Mr Ian Lester. Our searches indicated his last known address was at Gayvor Farm, Eastern Road, North Dorga. There doesn’t seem to be any landline connected to the property and we couldn’t identify a mobile phone registered to the man.”

"Aye, Ian Lester. He works as a labourer at Gayvor Farm, he's been there a good three year' now. They put him up in a static caravan on the site, although he's pretty much part of the family. He drinks at the pub with the sons on a Friday night, that kind of thing. The family are called Sinclair. They've farmed that land since forever."

Dan glanced at Tyler and raised his brows, pleased with this confirmation their onerous trip hadn't been in vain. "Great. If you could provide some directions, we will make our way out there."

Eddie gave another thin smile. "There are no buses on the island and the guys who run the taxis work their land in the day." He leant across to a coat stand in the corner, lifting off a bulky sheepskin jacket. "If you wait for me to grab the truck, I'll take you there myself."

Chapter 19

The infinite sky was grey and threatening. The cab of Eddie Shewan's beaten-up Toyota Hilux was untidy. Plastic cups were discarded in the footwells and piles of documents took up their own seat in the back.

Dan tried not to turn up his nose at the mess. He was a stickler for order and cleanliness himself. Instead, he kept his vision fixed on the landscape they were bumping past. Rolling hills were dotted with stone walls and the occasional cairn. Any trees to be seen were stunted and their branches wizened and curled in on themselves, like a bent old man against the rain.

The road had been tarmacked but there was barely room for two vehicles to pass. If this was typical of the main roads in North Dorga, Dan could see why it would be difficult to run a bus service. But then, outside of St Martin, there seemed little other evidence of human habitation. They'd barely passed a 'but 'n' ben', let alone many cottages. The island was one long strip of rugged coastline, with a few fields in between.

Eddie was giving his passengers a running commentary. "This is the eastern road, which runs along the coast until it reaches the lighthouse. There is no western road, so if you want to reach that stretch of coast you need to walk it, or take a sea kayak as many of the locals do. We've no other islands except to the south, so the wind rushes onto our shores straight from Norway. No flora here grows above four feet tall."

"What can you farm then, in these harsh conditions?" Tyler asked from the backseat.

"Fishing is the main business here, always has

been. The name 'Dorga' itself, is old Norse for fishing line. The farms tend to concentrate on cattle these days, although they all try to be self-sufficient food-wise too. South Dorga is even smaller. There's no police station, so DC Harvey and I are responsible for both, although there are barely a hundred inhabitants on our sister isle."

Dan tried to imagine an island even more bleak than this one. It wasn't easy. "What would a relatively young man like Ian Lester be doing all the way out here? It's hardly full of opportunities, is it?" Dan was careful not to be too condemnatory, aware the man seated beside him at the wheel was a resident of the island himself.

"You're city folk. It's hard for you to understand the way of life here. Ian seems to enjoy working on the land and with the animals. We barely have a Wi-Fi connection; no buses or trains. We like to feel as if we are free."

Tyler thought of his cosy flat back in Glasgow with his games consoles and latest iPhone. He looked out of the window and shuddered.

Dan was put in mind of the climate crisis activists like Earth's Saviours who were out in force on the streets of his home city during the two weeks of the conference. He supposed that the life led here on this tiny island was the ideal for them.

Eddie's words cut through his thoughts. "You say that Ian's father is dead?"

Dan nodded. "Aye, he was murdered in a hotel room at the COP26 conference. We need to inform Ian of the death and ask him a few questions. Although, the details are being kept from the press, for obvious reasons."

"You'd barely know the lad had family beyond the Sinclairs. He's never mentioned them."

"There's an older sister and his mother. Both are

still alive from what we can gather from the records. The entire family seem to have been estranged."

"It's an odd business."

A farmhouse appeared on a hillside to the left of them. Several run down barns were scattered around it and a gravelled road formed a straight line to the building's front door. Dan assumed this was Gayvor Farm. Eddie made an abrupt turn, the Hilux churning up the loose stones as it charged up the slope to the accompanying sound of chipping paintwork.

The detectives climbed out. Eddie strode confidently round to the side of the house, knocking on what looked like a kitchen door.

A woman with long, fairish hair, braided to her shoulders and wearing a thick cotton shirt and corduroy trousers opened up. An Airedale Terrier was weaving round her legs. "Eddie? What brings you up here today?" She glanced beyond the local policeman to the two strangers, smartly dressed. Her brow creased.

"We're here to speak with Ian Lester, Maggie. These men are police from Glasgow."

The woman clutched the dog's collar and stepped back into the dingy kitchen. "Come away in. He's up on the hill with Stevie. But they're due back for lunch any minute. You'd best wait for them."

Eddie took a seat at a large round table. The other officers did the same.

"Shall I make tea?" Maggie Sinclair asked warily.

"Aye, that's best," Eddie sighed. "These boys have got bad news for Ian."

Dan bristled at being described as a 'boy'. If they needed to conduct an investigation here, Eddie was undermining them with his dismissive language.

Tyler glanced at the coal-fired stove. A large pot on the burner was emitting a rich, meaty smell. Now he'd recovered from his sea-sickness, his stomach growled fiercely. They'd not eaten since dawn.

Maggie filled a kettle and placed it beside the pot before joining them at the table. "Has someone died?"

Dan jumped in before Eddie could confirm. "We really need to speak with Ian Lester before we provide any details, Madam."

She raised her eyebrows. "That's a yes then." She reached down to ruffle the curly fur on the dog's head. "Although, I don't know who it could be. Ian never mentions his family. We've sensed it's best not to press him on it."

"How long has Ian worked here for you?" Tyler asked.

Her eyes turned up to the ceiling as she considered this. "He arrived on the doorstep looking for work in the Summer of 2018. As it happened, we needed an extra pair of hands. Stevie was on the mainland at agricultural college back then. We cleaned up the caravan out back and he sleeps out there. But he's in the house for all his meals and joins us in the evening if he wants."

"Do you know where he was working before, Mrs Sinclair? Did his references provide an address?"

The woman's cheeks flushed pink. "We never asked for any. Labour is very scarce here on North Dorga. We took Ian on for a probationary period. That was three years ago, there has never been any problem with his work. I'd go as far as to say he's part of the family now."

Eddie nodded. "Shall I make that tea, Mags?"

"Aye, if you wouldn't mind. The mugs are in the cupboard."

Dan noted how familiar the local detective was with the family. "Does Ian take holidays? Go home for Christmas, that kind of thing?"

"Like I said, I don't believe there's any such thing as *home* for Ian. Except here of course. He's spent the last three Christmases with us."

Dan was about to ask more when the door swung open and two burly young men stepped into the kitchen, a gust of wind swirling in with them, like an unwanted guest. Both stood stock still when they spotted the detectives seated at the table.

Dan got to his feet. "Ian Lester?"

The second man moved forward, his hair was dark and shoulder-length, swept into a quiff by the blustery conditions outside. He was at least six foot tall and wore a battered waxed jacket and heavy boots. "That's me."

"I am DC Clifton from Police Scotland, based in Glasgow. May I speak with you in private?"

Chapter 20

Maggie Sinclair insisted she set the fire in the open grate of the front sitting room before the detectives could interview Ian in there.

The young man was perched on the edge of a high-backed tapestry sofa which was threadbare and heavily worn. His rough hands were clasped together in his lap and his head hung down, revealing the thick dark swirls of his crown.

As the flames began dancing up the chimney, Eddie Shewan entered with a tray of teas. He set Ian's on the coffee table in front of him. The young man didn't seem to notice.

The local detective took a chair by the door, but their hostess made a hasty retreat. Dan felt annoyed that Eddie was staying, although he knew his rancour wasn't really justified. This was his jurisdiction, after all.

Dan waited until the woman had closed the door gently behind her. "Can you confirm that you are Ian David Lester, born on 25th January 1994 in Inverness, to Quentin and Fiona Lester?"

The young man nodded dolefully.

This would have to do. They weren't in an official interview. "I'm sorry to have to inform you, Ian, that your father, Quentin Lester, was found dead in his hotel room in Glasgow on 1st November. We have been trying to locate you ever since to break the news. Your father was identified by his medical records."

Ian finally glanced up. His expression was one of absolute surprise. "Dad's *dead*?"

"I'm afraid so. The cause of death was a very serious heart attack." Dan was at least relieved not to have to elaborate on the manner of the man's demise at this stage.

"D-do I need to come and identify him?" The man stuttered.

"Not if you don't wish to. That was done via video link by his current employer as we couldn't locate a next of kin at the time."

Ian rubbed the stubble on his chin. "I haven't seen Dad in a few years. We never really got on very well. Actually, I thought he was living in Africa?"

The detectives exchanged glances.

"Your father returned from Tanzania in 2018," Tyler explained gently.

Ian reached for the mug of tea and slurped a mouthful. "Where's he been in the meantime?"

"He was working for a children's charity in Stirling. He was well regarded in his job, that's why he was chosen as a delegate for the climate conference."

Ian's vision skittered around the room before resting again on his lap, he appeared confused. "Dad was at the COP26 conference when he died?"

"Yes, he was discovered in his hotel room by security staff, when he didn't turn up for a seminar."

Dan shuffled forward in his seat. "We wouldn't have come all this way if your father had simply died of natural causes. From the way we discovered your father's body, it was clear the heart attack was brought on by a very violent attack. We have a murder team working on the case."

Ian began shaking his head vigorously. "None of this makes any sense."

Dan was surprised the young man wasn't more interested in the circumstances of his father's death. "Can you think of any reason why someone would want your father dead? Any enemies he had; arguments or disputes with people?"

Ian wrung his hands. "I told you, I'd not had any

contact with him since he went to Africa. That's over five years ago. I don't know anything about him."

"You must have had a pretty strong disagreement to have become so completely estranged?" It was Eddie who made this point.

Ian turned to the officer and replied. "Dad was very rigid, he wanted me and my sister to go to university and settle into an office job. It wasn't what either of us wanted. When we didn't do what he expected of us, he lost interest. There was no big argument."

"That would be Elinor, your older sister? We haven't been able to trace her yet, or your mother?" Dan asked.

"Mum lives in Edinburgh, she's got a husband and a new life. Elinor is now called Billi something. She changed her name by deed poll yonks ago, she hangs around with eco-types. She doesn't have a permanent address, so I wouldn't rate your chances of finding her."

"Does she have any links to the Earth's Saviours group? They are very high profile at the moment, what with the climate conference being hosted in Scotland."

He shrugged his shoulders. "I wouldn't know. Most of the folk she hangs about with are hippy types, doped up and away with the fairies. I don't expect any of them really know what it's like to make a living from the earth."

"If you could provide us with a name and address for your mother then, that would be most helpful."

"Yeah, sure." Ian waved his hand dismissively. "But don't expect her to give a shit Dad's dead. I don't suppose he's even crossed her mind in fifteen years."

Dan modulated his tone so it was soft, cajoling. "And what about you, Ian? Has your father crossed *your* mind in the last few years?"

The man before them sat up straight and made a rigid line with his mouth. "No, he hasn't. I don't think about any of them. I've a new life here now and I'm happy with it."

Dan watched him carefully; his posture was defiant, but the moisture just evident around his eyes revealed to the detective what he'd been told wasn't entirely the case.

*

The Hilux hurled along the eastern road, back towards St Martin; a fierce sheet of rain lashing the windscreen, causing the old wipers to creak against the strain.

"Where was Maggie's husband today?" Dan asked, raising his voice above the screech of the wiper blades.

"Roy would be out on deliveries. They've got a van that they fill with their sausages and steaks. The butchers in the village take most of it, but he'll deliver to some of the more out of the way houses too, away in the west."

"Does Ian get on well with Roy?"

"Aye, I'd definitely say so. He travels in the van wi' 'im sometimes, as does Stevie and their youngest, Joe. It seems to me that Ian has found himself another family he likes better than his old one."

Dan nodded in agreement, glancing out of the window at the darkening sky and curtain of rain. Ian Lester had travelled to the edge of the world to escape his old family, but fortune had smiled on him when he was taken in by a new one.

Would a difference in outlook really precipitate such a complete break between father and son? Dan had been in the job long enough to smell when there was something more. There was definitely another reason why this family went its separate ways. But the question was, did it have anything to do with Quentin Lester's murder? That was still as unclear as the current view out of Eddie Shewan's rain splattered windscreen.

Chapter 21

A group had gathered around Klara Laska's adopted workstation. Dermot had invited Alice, Sharon and the DCI to hear what the woman had so far discovered.

Klara had her laptop open, facing the officers. She began speaking, as if delivering a familiar seminar. "We cannot really use the term *modus operandi* in relation to the killer of Quentin Lester, as in criminology terms, it suggests a common methodology in the organisation and manner of a killing. So far, we only have one murder, therefore, we cannot attribute a pattern."

"But this person could have killed before, in a case outside our jurisdiction, or copied the MO of another perpetrator? It's so unusual for a murder scene to be 'dressed' in such an elaborate manner," Dani suggested.

Klara nodded. "Precisely, which is why I am here to perform the analysis of the data."

Sharon pulled out a wheelie chair and sat down with a bump, wishing this prim consultant would cut the lecture and deliver her results.

The analyst continued. "From the forensic and circumstantial evidence, it seemed to me that our killer is inexperienced; there was much preparation ahead of the crime, but in the heat of the attack, the stake did not penetrate the victim's heart and the gown was pulled onto the body hastily after death. They only narrowly escaped discovery by the security services. Yet the dressing of the scene indicates the perpetrator has a point they wish to make. I have the feeling this is the first murder they have committed, but not the last."

"So, have you found any matches with our MO?"

Alice was also trying to keep the frustration out of her tone.

Klara tapped at her keypad. A list appeared on the screen. "I examined the records for the whole of the UK over the past ten years. There have been multiple cases of fatal stabbings during this time, but the majority were gang related, or occurred on the streets of big cities as part of a robbery. Lester was not robbed of his possessions so I discounted those. I found no reference at all to academic gowns, black cloaks or any other similar item in conjunction with a violent death." Klara reached for a water bottle and took a sip. "Then I looked for stabbings with a cross-shaped object, or a wooden stake. There were a handful, which I have listed here."

"Can we have a copy of that list?" Dani asked.

"Sure, I will email them to you all," Klara replied. "In one case, a sharpened wooden post was driven into the chest of a man during a house party which had descended into a brawl. Another man was arrested at the scene and is now in prison."

"Sounds nasty, but nothing really like our case," Dermot added.

"No, I agree. Another man was stabbed with a letter opener which had an ecclesiastical cross pattern on the handle. The perpetrator was his wife, apparently after years of domestic abuse."

Dani was beginning to become frustrated, she was thinking about the discussion she'd had with Andy a couple of days before. "These cases don't really bear any resemblance to ours. Perhaps the dressing of the scene is a red-herring? Someone wants to confuse us with the mixed messaging of the cross and the gown, to lead us down a blind alley?"

"This is certainly possible," Klara continued. "But whatever the reason for the choice of MO, it still reveals something about our killer."

Alice had been scanning the list over the analyst's shoulder. "How about this case, it took place in Scotland a couple of years back? A woman in her late fifties was drowned in her bathtub."

"Yes," Klara interrupted, her tone indicating she didn't appreciate being pre-empted. "Mabel Flett, 58 years old, was discovered by her husband when he returned to their house in Caithness on 10th April 2017. The bathroom was awash with water, the woman was fully clothed, bent double over the tub with her face submerged. Death was by drowning. The reason it flagged up as a match with our murder is that her hands had been bound behind her back with strips of dried palm leaves which had cut into her skin as she struggled against her attacker. It turned out the strips had come from one of those palm crosses they give out in church services over Easter. There were no prints left at the scene. No sign of a break-in. The husband had an alibi. No arrest has ever been made."

Dani's interest was now piqued. "Have you got access to any crime scene photos?"

Klara nodded, opening an attachment and moving the laptop forward so the group could get a good view and flicking through the pictures like a slideshow.

Alice squinted her eyes at the images. "There was definitely one hell of a struggle, there's water all over the bathroom floor. I'm amazed there was enough left in the bath to drown her."

"It doesn't take much water to drown a person in," Sharon added levelly, "especially when you've got your face pressed down in it."

The DCI looked at Dermot. "You were the only one of us who saw the scene of Lester's murder. What do you think? Any connection?"

Dermot had been examining the pictures closely.

"There are signs of a significant struggle here, whereas at the Lester murder, almost none. In our case, the cross was the murder weapon, here it was used purely to restrain. The body in this case is fully clothed, yet Lester was naked except for the socks, shirt and gown. There were sexual overtones present in our case but not here, not from what I can see. I'd like to fully review the case notes though."

Alice sighed. "Are there any other matches in your list?"

Klara shook her head. "The remainder are stabbings with stake-like objects, in all cases a perpetrator was arrested and charged. But I can take these parameters back further than ten years?" She glanced at Dermot for his approval.

Abruptly, Sharon got to her feet and leant in closer to the screen, upsetting a cardboard cup with the dregs of a take-out coffee in it which dribbled onto a stack of documents. "What's that in the corner of the image? Can you zoom in for us?"

Klara raised her eyebrows at this ungainly outburst. "Okay. The left hand corner segment, yes?"

Sharon nodded vigorously.

The image became more pixelated at this magnification, but there was definitely an item visible to the side of the photograph; a blur of brown and red.

"What the hell is it?" Dani asked with interest.

"It's a teddy bear, Ma'am," Sharon replied. "With a bright red bow around its neck."

"Is it mentioned in the crime scene reports?" Dani directed her question at the analyst.

"Yes, it was found underneath the sink, to the right of the body. The Fletts had a couple of grandchildren and it was assumed to have belonged to one of them."

"Did the husband confirm this?" Dani snapped.

Klara shrugged. "I don't have access to all the files, I'm sorry."

Dani turned to Dermot. "Can you request those files from Highlands and Islands? Let's get a more detailed description of that crime scene. The murder took place in Caithness. We know Lester had connections to Inverness and the Orkneys, through his estranged son. It's worth checking this out further."

"So, what if the teddy bear didn't belong to the grandkids?" Alice asked her boss.

"Then it was a part of the killer's staging," Dani replied carefully. "I've got no idea how it could link to our murder, but I want to find out more before we discount it."

Chapter 22

The terrible weather hadn't let up. Dan stared out of the bay window of the only pub in St Martin, staring at the rain bouncing off the road outside and the boats bobbing in the bay.

Tyler carried a couple of pints to their table. "Don't tell me we're going to have to sail back to Kirkwall in *that.*"

Dan took a long sup of his lager. "No. The landlord told me the ferry won't run in these conditions. He's got a couple of spare rooms upstairs that I've booked for the night."

"Well, I'm relieved we aren't sailing in a storm, but to be honest, I'm not keen on spending much longer on this island." He lowered his voice to a rasp.

"Me neither. The internet connection comes and goes. I had to relay all the information we gathered from our interview with Ian Lester to DI Muir down the phone in the hallway. It's hardly the most confidential way to share evidence."

Tyler sipped his drink thoughtfully. "At least the team back at Pitt Street can track down Lester's ex-wife. We had a full name to give them."

"Yes, Fiona Black. According to Ian, she remarried in 2005 and lives in Colinton. Although, the address may be out of date, he wasn't sure."

Tyler shook his head. "I suppose I can understand Ian having a falling out with his dad. But why does he see so little of his mum, too? He's about my age. He's spending his youth living up there on that Godforsaken farm. I don't get it."

"Some folk don't get on with their families. I've got plenty of friends who haven't spoken with their parents since coming out. I was one of the lucky ones."

"Yeah, I get that. But do you reckon it was something like that with Ian? He said his dad was too strict and wanted him to be more academic, but maybe he's gay too and his dad didn't like it? He was of an older generation?"

Dan took several gulps of his drink. "It could be the case, but I certainly didn't pick up that vibe from Ian. In the cases of the people I know, as soon as they come out to their family they tend to head for the cities that have a thriving gay scene; where they will find like-minded people and be accepted; like Glasgow, London or Manchester." He glanced around at the old fashioned surroundings of the lounge bar, where the curtains had gold tassels and the wallpaper was a riot of velvet flock. "They certainly wouldn't come here."

Tyler laughed. "You've got that right. Although, it's so dated in this place it's almost kitsch."

Dan chuckled too. "Yeah, *almost*."

They finished the rest of their drinks in silence.

"Come on," Dan announced, placing his empty glass on the table. "Let's turn in and hope that conditions have improved by morning."

*

If the detectives were hoping for a break in the weather, they were to be disappointed. As Dan sat at the same table they'd occupied the previous night to a plate of bacon and eggs he looked out at the menacing sky that hung over the tiny port of St Martin.

The rain had stopped for the moment, but the wind was rattling the old frames of the building and a bitter draft had kept the detective awake for most of the night.

As Tyler slunk over to the table and dropped into the chair opposite, he didn't appear to have got much rest either.

"Bad night?" Dan poured a cup of mahogany brown tea for his colleague.

"The window in my room was banging all night from the wind and someone next door was snoring like a trooper."

"It wasn't me," Dan added indignantly.

"I think it was the bloody landlord. We ought to ask for a discount."

"Unfortunately, we need to keep him on side as he has the only accommodation on the island."

As if sensing his name had been taken in vain, the landlord entered the room with a notepad. He was a small man with a rounded stomach. "What can I get you for breakfast, son?"

Tyler looked out of the window at the angry sea and decided they wouldn't be getting on a boat that day. "A full Scottish, please."

The landlord nodded. "Lucky we got a delivery from Roy Sinclair yesterday."

Dan glanced up. "Do you get all your meat from Sinclair?"

"Aye, he's got a nice herd of cattle that he breeds for meat and a field of pigs for the sausages. Sometimes one o' the boys will go oot fishing an' there'll be a few herring in the van too. But I get most of ma' fish from Mainland. It comes over on tha' ferry. There's no' so many fishermen on the island any longer, what with the quotas and what have you."

"Do you know the Sinclairs well?" Dan persisted, thinking he might as well take advantage of their extra time here to dig for information.

"Ma' place is the only pub on the island. Roy, Stevie and Ian drink in here most weekends. Joe isn't old enough yet, but Mags brings him in sometimes for a coke. They're a good family. Been on Dorga for generations."

"Does Ian get on well with the family?"

"You wouldnae know he wasn't their own son." He narrowed his eyes. "The lad's no' in any trouble is he? Only, we've no' had polis from the mainland over here on Dorga in a long, long, time. Eddie and Tracey usually handle things just fine."

"No, he's not in any trouble at all." Dan smiled over his tea cup.

The landlord looked unconvinced. "Right, I'd best get your fry-up on the go then."

Chapter 23

One of the DCs had brought a tray full of takeout coffees into the department. It was clear to Dani that the DCS was trying to make her murder teams' lives as easy as possible in order to get a quick result. She knew it didn't quite work that way, but was grateful for any perks her officers were given.

Alice grabbed a couple of the cardboard cups and carried one over to the DCI's office, where her door was left ajar. "I thought you might want one of these, Ma'am. Courtesy of DCS Douglas."

Dani nodded, glancing up from her pile of paperwork. "Pop it on my desk, thanks."

"I've just come off the phone from Fiona Black, the lady Dan informed us was Quentin Lester's ex-wife."

Dani gave the officer her full attention. "Oh yes? What did she have to say for herself?"

"Fiona Black re-married in 2005. She and her new husband live in Colinton, Edinburgh. She works as a nurse at the infirmary. Mrs Black has had no contact with Lester since he returned from Africa in 2018. On the day Lester was murdered, she was working a day shift at the hospital, which will be easy enough for us to check."

Dani sighed, reaching for the cup of coffee and blowing away the steam rising from it. "So, his estranged son is ensconced on a farm on an island that's ten hours journey from here and his ex-wife has a cast iron alibi for the time of Lester's death. Did she give you any idea why none of them had anything to do with our victim?"

"According to her, Quentin was a miserable old bully. He was always nagging her and the kids.

Finally, she plucked up the courage to leave him and she says they've never been happier without him in their lives."

"Was she not at all upset by the news of his death?" Dani sipped the bitter coffee.

"I'd say she was genuinely surprised, but not upset."

Dani shook her head. "It sounds like Lester was a difficult man to live with. I'm sure he was overbearing and pushy with his kids. But to completely cut him out of their lives? Usually, there's a stronger catalyst for such an acrimonious family estrangement."

"I agree," Alice said. "Dan suggested the son, Ian Lester, has not told them the whole story about his relationship with his dad."

"When are he and DC Sullivan returning?"

"The weather is still too unsettled for a boat to take them back to Mainland Orkney. Dan says they're going to use the time to find out more about the lad."

"Okay, it's not ideal losing two of my team for all this time, but perhaps they can dig up something useful from Ian Lester."

"I did get something else of interest from Fiona Black."

Dani raised her eyebrows. "Oh yes?"

"She is in occasional contact with her daughter, previously known as Elinor Lester, who has changed her name to Billi Star and is an active campaigner for environmental issues."

Dani put down her cup. "Is the daughter involved with Earth's Saviours?"

"Fiona wasn't sure. She says Billi travels around a lot, sleeps on friends' sofas and joins whatever protests happen to be going on at the time. She works in pubs or serving food in cafés on temporary contracts in order to fund her lifestyle."

"Does Fiona know her daughter's current whereabouts?"

"She hadn't spoken to her in a couple of weeks, at that time her daughter had been staying with a friend in Tollcross."

Dani's eyes lit up. "Then this Billi Star has been in Glasgow? If she's an environmental activist, she *must* be involved in the COP26 demos. It's the biggest thing to have happened in the world of environmentalism since Greenham Common."

"Aye, there must be a connection."

"Get onto your contact from Earth's Saviours. Let's see if she's heard of the woman. We need to track down Billi Star and see if *she's* got an alibi for the day her dad was killed."

Alice nodded, leaving the office with the coffee cup gripped in her hand, determined to follow up this new lead.

*

Alice placed her mobile phone on the desk with a clatter. Sharon looked up from her screen. "Any joy with Macy McAdams?"

Alice sighed heavily. "She hasn't heard of anyone calling themselves, Billi Star. But she also says they have dozens of extra volunteers who've joined up during the conference. Their headquarters are full of folk making banners and planning demos, at least a half of them Macy hasn't ever seen before."

"Don't they have some kind of enrolment programme? They must have a register of volunteers' names?"

Alice chuckled. "I don't think the set-up is as organised as that, Sharon. To make the most of the publicity around COP26, I sense it's all hands on deck. Macy barely had time to talk to me, she was about to leave for a demonstration in George Square. They are going to be addressed by Tiger Sampson, the head of the scout movement and well-known survivalist."

"We might just find Billi Star at that demonstration."

"Yes, along with several thousand others, all dressed the same."

Sharon grimaced. "The mother's description *was* fairly generic; early thirties, cropped, dyed hair, hippie-style clothing."

"Apparently, Billi's hair colour changes by the day. She doesn't have a passport or a driving licence, so there's nothing we can use as a basis for a search. With such an airy-fairy description, we can't even ask Andy's team to keep an eye out for her."

Sharon crossed her arms over her chest. "But Lester's daughter was very likely in Glasgow when he was killed. She's probably connected to Earth's Saviours, and the murder weapon was a symbol of the group. This is the closest thing we've got to a lead. We've got to do *something* to try and track her down."

Alice grabbed her jacket from the back of her chair. "You're absolutely right, Sharon. Let's go."

Chapter 24

The wind was hurling stinging sea-spray into their faces as the two detectives trekked towards the St Martin police station, their padded coats zipped up to their chins.

Dan pushed through the entrance door, feeling his body relax as it encountered a wall of heat. Tyler closed the door resolutely behind them, leaving the howling gale firmly on the outside.

"*Jeez, that bloody weather,*" Tyler muttered bitterly, as he shrugged out of his sodden coat and placed it on a hook.

Dan did the same, ruffling the rainwater out of his long fringe.

Eddie Shewan stepped towards the reception desk, lifting a hatch for them to enter the office area. "I've put the blowers on for you," he said amiably. "I've also put the coffee machine on to percolate. I thought we may need some artificial stimulation."

Dan smiled gratefully, noticing for the first time a woman seated at one of the desks. She was dressed in a navy ribbed jumper and combat trousers, her brown hair shoulder-length; she appeared to be in her late thirties, a few years Eddie's junior.

"DC Tracey Harvey is on duty with me today. We always get a few callouts when the wind is up like this; usually fences down and cattle escaped, that kind of thing. But it often requires the two of us."

Dan moved across the room and offered her his hand. "I'm DC Dan Clifton and this is DC Tyler Sullivan. We appreciate you letting us use your station like this."

The woman accepted his handshake, her grip was firm. "No problem. I often miss working as part of a team. I was based on Kirkwall for a few years before I came back here."

"Are you local to Dorga?" Dan asked conversationally.

"Oh, aye, most of us who stay on the island were born and bred here. It's a difficult place to adjust to otherwise." Tracey accepted a mug of coffee from her colleague. "We do have some settlers, of course. But the English tend to buy on Mainland, where there are more services."

"Is there a school on Dorga?" Tyler asked, sitting in one of the chairs and cradling his warm mug, feeling his numb fingers start to tingle.

"There's a primary here on the north island," Tracey explained. "there aren't any children on the south island at the moment, but if there were, they would take the boat over and back, weather permitting." She glanced out of the window at the water streaking down the murky pane and gave an ironic lift of an eyebrow.

"What about secondary?" Tyler prompted.

"There isn't one here. When I was younger, I stayed with my auntie on Mainland to attend the High School there. A few of my contemporaries did the same; bunking up with relatives or friends. But these days, the young ones go over once a month for a teaching day and they bring work back with them to the island. When the Wi-Fi is playing ball, they can keep in contact with teachers online."

Tyler thought this was a lonely and isolated existence for a teenager, but he didn't say so.

As if he could sense the detective's scepticism, Eddie added, "We've a couple of dozen teens here on Dorga. I run a football team and there are plenty of other activities going on. We have a strong community spirit which is lacking in many of the big cities."

Dan nodded. Small communities had never been

his cup of tea, largely because it could be difficult to be gay in such places, which often encouraged more old-fashioned sensibilities. But he knew that times had moved on and was sure Dorga was as progressive as anywhere on the mainland these days. "Do you know Ian Lester?" He asked the female detective.

"A little. My partner serves behind the bar in the pub. He knows him to speak to. The man is friendly enough."

"The Sinclair's younger son, Joe, is on my football team. He's studying for his Highers. One of the kids who get ferried over once a month to the Mainland High School," Eddie explained.

"There's quite an age gap between him and Stevie, then?" Dan pointed out.

"Aye, Joe was a late arrival, something of a surprise, I reckon." Eddie sipped from his mug.

"Would it have been possible that Ian could've left the island for a few days last week without being noticed?" Dan voiced the question that had been circling in his mind since the previous day.

Eddie put down his mug. "The weather was fairly stable last week, so the ferries were running, but it's only old Lonny in his boat. If Ian had left the island, he'll be the man to ask."

Dan made a mental note to do so. "Where can we find Lonny when the ferry isn't running?"

It was Tracey who answered. "He'll be propping up the bar in the pub most evenings. My Mick says he's a permanent fixture. Lonny isn't a difficult man to track down."

The phone on Eddie's desk began to ring. He picked it up, listening intently. "Aye, I understand. We'll be there as soon as we can with the truck." He put down the receiver and turned to his fellow officers. "A bull has slid down a bank and got itself stuck in a burn up at Gayvor Farm; the Sinclairs' place. I'll sling a rope in the back of the truck. We can pick up the vet on the way."

Tracey sprung to her feet, reaching for a waxed jacket draped over the chair beside her.

Dan rose in unison, "We'll come and help." He fell into step purposefully behind Tracey Harvey, ignoring the look of undisguised annoyance on Tyler's face.

Chapter 25

The air was crisp and cold but the sky was a clear cornflower blue. The autumn sun was shining onto the platform that had been erected in front of the municipal chambers in George Square.

Alice and Sharon joined the throngs of people jostling to get as close as possible to the man who was standing behind a microphone on the stage, his voice amplified to the crowd through a pair of enormous speakers. Tiger Sampson struck a surprisingly diminutive figure to the DI, who always felt he'd appeared larger than life on the TV.

The statues of Sir Walter Scott and Sir Robert Peel had been cordoned off with barriers, and one of their colleagues was positioned beneath each of them, a lonely bulwark against the swelling melee.

"Do you really think we're going to spot Billi Star in all these crowds?" Sharon raised her voice against the din.

"Not really, but at least we can be confident Quentin Lester's daughter is here somewhere. That's as close as we've come to a suspect since the man was murdered."

Alice observed the sea of wooden crosses being held up by the contingent from Earth's Saviours. Then she noticed Andy Calder's group of officers, who were forming a line at the edge of the green, conspicuous in their high-vis jackets. She nudged Sharon's arm and they elbowed their way towards them.

Andy had taken up a rigid stance at the head of his team. When he spotted Alice, his face creased into a wry smile. "I thought the boss had you focused on this murder inquiry?"

Alice shrugged. "Our investigations have brought us here. Has there been any trouble?"

Andy shook his head. "The protestors have remained very disciplined. This Sampson guy has some of his scouts up on stage reading out data about the state of the planet. Nobody wants to be guilty of bringing violence to the proceedings. But as you can see, the crowds are building. Even though we've got plenty of officers here, that feeling of being outnumbered always makes me nervous."

Alice felt the mob surge against her back and she shuddered. It only took a tiny incident; a flashpoint of fear, to turn this kind of mass gathering into a deadly stampede. But the atmosphere did feel friendly. For the time being. The man on stage was saying what those gathered wanted to hear.

Andy pointed into the distance. "The Earth's Saviours lot are over there, by Queen Street Station. You can see the heads of the crosses, bobbing above the crowd. To me, it looks like they're heading off on a crusade, about a thousand years too late."

Alice imagined it was a crusade of sorts for them. "Thanks Andy, we'll head in that direction."

Sharon took the lead, she had a way of broadening her shoulders and ploughing with ease through the throng, the slighter figure of her colleague being swept along behind. They finally reached the troupe of Earth's Saviours members. The crosses and banners seemed to number in their hundreds. A few children were visible amongst the multitudes, gripping an adult's hand and perhaps a small placard of their own, calling for the earth to be saved for their futures. Alice tried to imagine bringing Charlie to such an event when he was older, but couldn't picture it.

Alice scanned the faces of the protestors, not entirely sure what she was looking for. She found herself beside a woman who appeared to be in her late twenties. Her nose was pierced and her plaited hair dyed a rainbow of colours. "I'm looking for someone called, Billi Star," she ventured. "Do you know her?"

The woman shook her head, turning back in the direction of the stage.

Alice noticed Sharon was asking others the same question, nudging her way along the lines of protestors, who seemed prepared to create a path for her. As the detectives covered more ground, a sense of unease seemed to ripple through the lines of people around them.

Abruptly, Alice saw a disturbance in the crowd up ahead. Someone was shoving their way out through the ranks of the Earth's Saviours' contingent. She grabbed Sharon's sleeve and dipped her head in the direction of the commotion. Both officers began weaving their way towards whoever it was who'd decided to make a quick exit.

It felt to Alice like swimming through treacle; bodies were pressing against hers and making it hard to breathe. Hands pushing and shoving, elbows clashing with her face. Finally, she broke out onto a pavement where the numbers of people had thinned out. She gulped in the crisp air, glancing about her, noticing a flash of bright vermillion heading for the station entrance. She broke into a run, not even quite sure what she was chasing.

Suddenly, Sharon was by her side. "Did you see her? It was a woman with red hair, she had on one of those green smocks they wear. She was pushing her way out of the crowd, desperate to get away."

"Which way did she go?" Alice had reached the station concourse, scanning the area intently.

Sharon jogged towards the platforms, asking one of the station guards if they'd seen a woman with red hair enter the station. He shook his head.

Alice reached for her phone to call in the sighting. If it was Billi Star who had caught wind someone was asking for her amongst the people in the crowd and made a run for it, her image would've been captured on one of the many CCTV cameras that were trained on George Square and positioned in the station itself. If the woman had got on a train, they should be able to trace exactly where she was going.

Chapter 26

Tyler had never seen mud like it. The continuous rainfall had created a slick of peaty sludge that was creeping down the steep hillside towards a free-flowing, over-filled burn.

The Sinclairs' bull had clearly lost its footing as the ground became saturated and its considerable weight had caused it to slide down into the cold waters of the burn below, which were now lapping up to its flank. Eddie and the vet wasted no time in wading through the torrent to reach the stranded animal. Tracey Harvey shouted instructions from the waterlogged slope.

Dan and Tyler observed from the bank as the men secured a rope around the bull's neck and front legs and gently but firmly, led the impressive beast through the gushing waters. After a few metres, they reached a bank with a lesser gradient than the one the animal had slid down.

It then took the might of all four officers, plus Stevie Sinclair and Ian Lester, to guide the bull up the path and into a small barn on the edge of the field. There were moments when Tyler thought they might give up, when the bull, naturally frightened and cold, had reared up and resisted the pull of its handlers. But the farmers calmly persisted, patting and cajoling their animal until it gradually followed them towards safety.

When the bull was securely in the barn, under the care of the vet, Tyler stood on the edge of the field, staring up at the steel grey sky, with freezing rain running down the neck of his jacket and mud smeared over his trousers and caking his boots. He was shivering with both the exertion and the cold, a mixture of sweat and mud dripping down his face.

Stevie clapped him on the back. “You’d best come to the farmhouse,” he declared. “You’ll need to warm up too, just like Gordie.”

Tyler imagined Gordie was the bull, who was hopefully none the worse for his dunking in the burn. Eddie volunteered to stay with the vet and give him any assistance he required, Tracey wanted to check on the remainder of the herd. but the two officers didn’t object when Stevie and Ian led them down towards the farmhouse and the promise of shelter from the merciless weather.

*

Maggie Sinclair had lit the fire in the front sitting room again. She insisted the two officers take a warm shower and dress in some spare clothes of her sons’. Dan didn’t object, he knew his clothing was ruined and just hoped the coat could be salvaged, otherwise he’d have no protection against the conditions they were currently enduring. He’d certainly not noticed any sign of an outdoor shop in St Martin where he could buy a new one.

Dan came down the stairs twenty minutes later, towel drying his hair, wishing he had some of his usual products with him. He found Tyler seated on the sofa, wearing a fair isle jumper and jogging bottoms, cradling a mug of tea, his buzz cut not requiring much maintenance.

“Yours is on the table,” the young detective commented.

“Thanks.” Dan dropped onto the seat beside him and reached for the mug eagerly. “I hope Eddie’s okay out there. He and the vet went in the water, they’ll be soaked to the skin.”

“He seems more used to the conditions than we are.” Tyler took a sip of the scalding tea, grateful for the heat it provided as it slipped down his throat. “Besides, Roy Sinclair came back from his deliveries.

He's gone over to help them."

Maggie came to stand in the doorway. "I've put your clothes in the machine, I hope you don't mind. I'm used to doing the lads' muddy work gear, so it makes no odds to have a few more."

"Thank you very much, Mrs Sinclair. You've been very generous," Dan answered sincerely.

Maggie shook her head. "Stevie said it took all of you to get Gordie back up that hill. We couldn't have shifted him without your help. He seems to be doing okay now. The vet's giving him some antibiotics in case he's caught a chill, but he's warm enough where he is."

"Good," Tyler said with feeling, surprised how interested he was in the welfare of the animal.

"Gordie is our top bull," Maggie continued. "He has bred all of our best calves for the last few years. If something happens to him, he would be a fortune to replace. I don't think the business would survive it."

Dan nodded, beginning to understand the precarious nature of farming in such a remote location. "Well, I'm just relieved we got him to safety."

"Eddie is a great help to us, and Tracey too. They do far more than just police this island."

"I'm starting to realise that," Dan said with a wry grin.

Maggie perched on the arm of a chair. "The winters here can be very tough. The ferry often can't sail and the hours of daylight are short. We need to be able to pull together as a community, to trust one another. If we aren't able to do that, the entire island suffers."

Dan somehow felt as if the woman were speaking from experience. He was about to ask her more, when Ian emerged from the hallway, dressed from head to foot in waterproofs. "I'm taking the Land Rover up to the point, to check on old Hugh. His place is always freezing, even without this wind."

Maggie nodded. "Okay, Ian. But don't be too long, now. Roy will need your help getting the entire herd into the barns. This weather is only set to get worse."

"Aye, I won't be long, I promise."

The young man rushed from the room.

Maggie shook her head, forming her mouth into a tolerant smile. "He's too soft for his own good, that one."

Dan placed his empty mug on the table. "You mentioned that the forecast was bad. Does that mean there won't be a ferry again tomorrow?"

Maggie was about to reply when she was interrupted by the noise of people entering through the kitchen door. She got to her feet. "That will be the others back. I'd best get a brew on for them too, they'll be cold and wet." With that, she bustled out of the room, leaving the detectives alone to exchange loaded glances. Both suspecting they weren't getting off the island any time soon.

Chapter 27

"If you're trying to be inconspicuous, it isn't a great idea to dye your hair that colour." Dermot was examining the CCTV footage that Alice had requested from Scotrail and Glasgow City Council.

"We are lucky that security is set to its highest level in the city right now, otherwise we may not have got this footage sent to us so quickly." Alice turned the screen so that her colleagues could get a good view of the images.

Dani sighed. "We don't want to have to rely too much on luck in this case. It has a nasty habit of running out."

Alice continued, unperturbed. "You can see our suspect here, breaking away from the crowd of Earth's Saviours demonstrators. She then heads toward the entrance to Queen Street Station."

"Yes, the red hair is really quite distinctive." Dani furrowed her brow. "Are we certain this woman is Elinor Lester, now calling herself, Billi Star?"

Sharon answered. "We were asking for Billi Star amongst the other protestors, I reckon people were talking about it in the crowd and the news reached her before we did. If she wasn't Billi, why would she run like that?"

"We won't know until we find her," Dermot added levelly.

"Which leads us on to the next image we have," Alice forwarded the recording. "The suspect proceeds straight to platform six. The 14.09 train to Balloch is about to depart and she gets on it."

Dermot nods. "Yep, I see that."

Alice clicked on a different file. "And there she is, getting off the train at the platform of Garscadden Station at 14.24pm. I've sent a couple of DCs over there to take a look. If she lives around there and needs to go to the shops or back to the station she won't be hard to spot."

"But we don't actually know she lives there?" Dani said. "If she knew she was being followed, she may have got off at Garscadden to throw you off the scent?"

Alice knew this question was coming. "Well, we don't have anything on our records relating to a Billi Star, or Elinor Lester; no tax information or DVLA licence. It seems to be as her brother said, she moves from place to place, probably working for cash-in-hand. I've checked the CCTV at the station for the next couple of hours to see if she got back on a train. There's no sign of her. I also checked the bus stops. No sign of her there either. She doesn't drive, so I reckon she's staying with someone local to that area."

Dani nodded. "Okay, that's a reasonable assumption. But the woman looks young and fit from these images, she could have walked a reasonable distance from there to get to wherever she calls home."

"I know it's a long shot, Ma'am. But at least we know what she looks like now, and we know she doesn't want to be found, which means she's got something to hide."

Dani wasn't sure that was always the reason why people didn't want to be found. Sometimes they were frightened of officials, or had bad experiences with the police in their pasts, but she had to concede that Alice and Sharon had got the closest to identifying Quentin Lester's daughter. "Okay, keep me posted on what the DCs report back. Dermot, can I have a word in my office?"

The DI followed his boss across the floor to her corner office, closing the door gently behind him.

Dani gestured for him to take a seat. "Did you receive the case notes from Highlands and Islands?"

"Yes, Ma'am. They were sent this morning. I've had a brief read through them." Dermot summoned up the documents on his tablet.

"I've no idea if this case has any bearing on ours so I didn't see any point in tying up the rest of the team with it."

"I agree. But the files are certainly intriguing. Mabel and Eric Flett lived in a semi-detached house in the Janetstown area of Wick, Caithness. Mabel was an administrator for the council and Eric had retired. They had two adult children who lived within a few miles of them and three grandchildren."

"The grandchildren were mentioned in the analyst's report."

"The murder took place on Monday 10th April 2017. It was Mabel's day off and Eric had gone to play golf with a friend who was also retired. There are witnesses who swear they were with him the entire day. The *PM* suggested the time of death was around noon. The immediate neighbours were out at work and nobody else on the street noticed anyone approaching or leaving the house."

"It was the middle of the day, on a suburban street. You'd think someone would've seen something?" Dani shook her head.

"The house backed onto fields, the garden ended in a low fence, so the killer could have approached that way, according to the detectives running the case. But there was no sign of a break-in."

"Mrs Flett let this person into her house. Would you open the door to someone who came round the back of your property?" Dani frowned.

"It would depend on who it was."

"True. It suggests perhaps she knew her killer?"

"Or they had an appointment? A tradesman

maybe? Although, Mr Flett insists they weren't expecting anyone and didn't need any work doing on the house."

"So, someone arrived at the house late morning, and Mrs Flett let them in?"

"There were no unidentified fingerprints in the property. No real signs of a struggle, except in the bathroom itself. It seems the killer forced Mrs Flett upstairs, bound her hands, ran the bath and then held her head under the water until she drowned. They were either wearing gloves the entire time, or did a good job of wiping down surfaces afterwards, although the tech reports showed Mr and Mrs Flett's prints everywhere; on doors and handles, so that seems unlikely."

"The killer must have had a weapon, to be able to overpower his victim like that, make her go upstairs without a fuss and wait whilst he ran a bath. Was Flett a small woman?"

"Not particularly, she was five foot five and slightly overweight, but no health conditions. I reckon she could have put up a fight."

"She struggled during the drowning itself, hence the gouge marks on the wrists and the water on the floor."

"I expect that's an automatic response, to struggle when you are drowning, trying to lift your head out of the water."

Dani shuddered, trying not to think about the woman's final moments. "What about the teddy bear? Did the husband recognise it?"

Dermot shook his head. "I specifically asked the officers at Highlands and Islands about this. Eric Flett was insistent he'd never seen the teddy before and the children confirmed it didn't belong to any of the grandchildren. The team wondered if Mrs Flett had bought it that morning and was going to give it to one of her grandchildren at a later date. But there's no evidence she went out, or even where she bought it. Online perhaps? But then a delivery driver might have come forward, which they never did. There would be payment records on her account." Dermot scratched his head, "and another thing was strange. Although it was sitting right near the bath, underneath the basin, the teddy was bone dry."

Dani felt a jolt of unease. "It was placed there *after* Mrs Flett had been killed, otherwise, it would have been soaked in the bathwater that was dislodged during the struggle."

"Yep, I think we can definitely say it was positioned there by the killer. But the question is *why*?"

"Why, indeed." Dani considered this for a moment. "And the palm cross which was used to bind the victim's hands? Where did that come from?"

"It had been Easter Sunday the day before. Mr and Mrs Flett had both been to a service at the local church where the crosses had been given out. There had been a couple in a jar by the kitchen door. One was missing."

"So, the teddy was brought by the killer, but the cross was opportunistic?" Dani sighed. "That doesn't help us. The cross is the only connection to our murder."

Dermot leant forward in his seat. "I think there must be more to the use of the cross. I mean, there are better ways to bind someone's hands, surely? Even a scarf or a belt would've been more effective. But with the cross the killer had to unravel the weave, it must have taken time. It was an added risk. No, I'm sure the cross was significant to the murderer."

Dani nodded slowly. "But nobody was ever arrested for the crime, no suspects even?"

“Nothing was taken from the house, so it didn’t seem like a robbery, there were no signs of sexual assault. Mrs Flett was a well-regarded grandmother. No motive to want her dead. The husband had an alibi and so had the family. The investigating team assumed it had to be an intruder unknown to the victim, but never got close to identifying who. There were no forensic clues and no witnesses.”

“There must have been a motive. For a crime so carefully staged and pre-prepared.”

“You could say exactly the same about the murder of Quentin Lester. We don’t have a motive for that yet, either.”

“No, and something tells me that when we do find out what it was, we might know why someone killed Mabel Flett, too.”

Chapter 28

Alice pressed the buzzer hard on the entry panel of the office building where the Earth's Saviours had their Glasgow headquarters. They heard the latch unclick within seconds. Macy McAdams knew they were coming.

The detectives took the lift to the top floor, this time knowing exactly where they were going. The open-plan loft space was even busier than when they had last paid a visit. People were milling about the vast space; constructing banners and having loud discussions.

When Macy approached them, she appeared stressed. "Follow me to the meditation space," she shouted above the noise. "It's just about the only place to get any peace."

The detectives followed, this time they didn't take a seat and Macy herself remained standing.

Alice pulled a file out of her bag. She found one of the stills they'd taken from the CCTV footage and showed it to the group leader. "We believe this woman is calling herself, Billi Star. She was standing amongst the Earth's Saviours protestors yesterday in George Square. We are keen to question her in connection with our investigation. Have you seen her before?"

Macy took the sheet and examined it closely. "I can't really see her face properly. I don't think I could say for sure."

"But look at the colour of her hair," Sharon exclaimed. "Surely you'd remember that?"

Macy gave a weary smile, gesturing around her. "We have a rainbow of colours to choose from in this very room. Many of our members have dyed their hair specifically for the duration of the conference, to show solidarity with the cause. I'm afraid it's not the distinguishing feature you think it is. Not in these circles anyway. If she's trying to evade you guys, I expect it's a different colour by now anyway."

Alice felt her heart sink. The woman was probably right. "But the name doesn't ring any bells? Or the name, Elinor Lester?"

"As I told you already, neither of those names appear on our members' register. But as you can see, our numbers have swelled considerably since the conference began. I didn't recognise half of the people who joined us at the protest yesterday." She raised her hands in frustration. "We want to encourage as many people as possible to join the cause. It's the point of this entire exercise!"

Alice thought perhaps she was regretting their success, judging by how harassed the woman was looking. "Okay, I get that. But can we ask around the building, see if someone else here recognises her?" She lowered her voice. "We are investigating a *murder*, after all?"

Macy sounded defeated. "Sure, ask away. But please be discreet about the reasons. I don't want our connection to this murder reaching the press."

Alice nodded, biting back a comment, just grateful the woman was being cooperative.

*

After an hour of interviewing, Alice and Sharon re-convened by the lift.

"Any luck?" Alice asked.

Sharon shook her notebook. "I've taken down a few names of people who think they saw our suspect yesterday, but nobody who really recognised the name or claims to know her well."

Alice scowled. "Same here. I don't really think Billi Star is a serious member of this group, they'd know her better if she was."

"I agree." Sharon pressed the button to summon the lift.

They waited in silence for it to arrive. Alice stepped in first and selected the button for the ground floor, the doors shuddering closed behind Sharon. But unlike the last time they visited, a light flickered onto the panel and the lift slowed at one of the lower floors, coming to a halt, the doors pinging open.

Alice looked up as a neatly dressed woman, with chestnut hair twisted into a bun at the base of the neck, joined them in the cab. She gave the officers a brief smile. An unpleasant, prickling feeling crept up Alice's spine. As the doors closed, her chest tightened in reaction to the close proximity of this woman, who stood with her back to the detectives, as still as a mannequin.

When they reached the ground floor, the woman stepped brusquely onto the tiles of the foyer, her low heels clicking out a steady rhythm as she crossed the echoey space and opened the door onto Church Street.

Alice found herself following the woman out of the door. She stood on the pavement, watching the slight figure walk in the direction of the city centre, her heart pounding in her chest and sweat forming on her brow despite the cold chill of the air.

Sharon came to stand beside her. "Are you okay?"

Alice nodded. "Yeah, I just think I know that woman, the one who got into the lift with us. I've seen her before, spoken to her even, but I've got no idea what she might be doing here."

Chapter 29

It wasn't long after Dan and Tyler's evening meal was cleared away that the landlord slipped behind the dark mahogany bar and started flicking on the lights above an impressive row of optics.

The detectives didn't wish to retire to their dingy rooms at such an early hour so decided to move onto a pair of padded bar stools and order a half pint each. By the time their drinks arrived, a steady stream of locals had pushed through the doors, letting in gusts of swirling rain behind them, graduating towards the empty tables and booths.

"I suppose there's not much else to do but go to the pub of an evening," Tyler muttered to his colleague.

Dan smiled into his beer glass. "Particularly when the weather's like this."

A man that looked to be in his thirties, wearing a plaid shirt and cords, with a thick head of unruly curls joined the landlord behind the bar.

Dan wondered if this was the partner of Tracey Harvey, whom she said worked at the pub. His suspicions were confirmed when a customer approached the bar and spoke with the barman. "Evening, Mick. I hear your missus helped shift the Sinclairs' bull from the burn this afternoon?"

Mick nodded, drawing the man a pint of stout from one of the pumps, without even asking what he wanted. "Aye, the water was up to its shoulders, the burn about to breach its banks. Once the animal got tired, it would've been a goner." He set down the glass of opaque liquid. "But these two fellas could tell you more," he dipped his head towards Dan and Tyler. "They were up at the farm too."

Dan supposed it was no surprise they were so

easily identifiable. “Yes, we were. The conditions were terrible.”

The local man eyed them carefully. “You’re the two polis from Glasgow?”

Dan nodded, taking a long sup of his drink. “Aye, we’re meant to be heading back, but the weather means the boat can’t sail.”

“This storm’s set to stay for a while,” he commented gloomily. “But we’re used to that kind of thing here.” He downed half his pint in one. “As long as we’ve got plenty of beer and whisky, we’ll be okay.”

“I had a delivery last week,” the landlord called over. “No worries on that score, Ciaran.”

The older man chuckled.

Tyler sighed into his glass.

Dan patted him on the shoulder. “We’ll be back soon enough.”

“He’s a young lad,” Mick said levelly. “Not wanting to be stuck on this wee island.”

“I wasn’t meaning to be disrespectful,” Tyler added quickly. “I’m just keen to get back to work, that’s all.”

“And probably to a pretty wee gal back in the city too, I don’t wonder?” This comment was met with further laughs.

Tyler took it in good humour.

“There are other young folk here on Dorga though?” Dan suggested, “Eddie was telling us he runs a few sports teams for local teenagers?”

Mick leant his muscly elbows on the bar. “Aye, there’s a handful of youngsters. But as soon as they reach a certain age, they’re away to Mainland and then off to uni somewhere, if they know what’s good for them.”

“Are you not so keen on the island, then?” Tyler asked.

Mick shrugged. "It's a beautiful place, but I'm on Dorga mainly because of Tracey. She was born and bred here. We met when she was based at Kirkwall, but she always wanted to come back. I knew that when we got together, can't complain."

"But there are settlers here, from other places?"

Mick and the local man exchanged glances. "The English prefer the larger islands, we've not had so many buying up the old farms here. But I expect that time may come."

"There's old Hugh, up by the lighthouse," the landlord offered.

"Oh aye," the local man said. "I'd forgot he were English, been on Dorga so long now."

Dan recalled this was the man Ian Lester had gone to visit earlier that day. "Does Hugh live on his own up there?"

The local man narrowed his eyes warily, emptying the remaining contents of his glass down his throat. "Aye, his wife passed away a few years back. The house has fallen into disrepair to be frank. I think Hugh lost the will to deal with the property a long time ago. It's a shame, 'cause it should've been a good, solid family home. That was always the intention, I reckon."

Dan was about to ask where the rest of Hugh's family were when the landlord reached across to grasp Ciaran's empty glass. "Will I fill this up again for you? Now, let's introduce these young visitors to some of our local whisky. No need to dwell on this maudlin stuff tonight."

*

When Dan laid his head on the down-filled pillow in his bedroom that night, the tiny room was spinning. He moaned quietly at his stupidity in accepting one too many whisky chasers. Tyler had seemed more sensible, switching to cokes at one point in the evening. He wondered if they were technically still on duty even, as they'd not been able to leave the island when intended.

Dan heard a faint knock at his door. He managed to call out, "come in!" before a wave of nausea and dizziness struck.

He opened his eyes to a slit and saw Tyler enter with a pint glass full of water. "The landlord thought you might want this." He placed it on the bedside table.

"Thanks. That's exactly what I need."

"That whisky was strong stuff. I'm not really a fan myself."

"Very sensible. I'm going to feel like shit in the morning. Don't tell the DCI, will you?"

"Course not. Besides, drinking with the locals helps them open up to you." Tyler perched on the end of the bed, the motion causing Dan's stomach to lurch.

"Which is not much good if you can't recall what they tell you."

"I bumped into Lonny, the ferryman, on my way to the toilet. He said Ian's not been on his boat for at least twelve months. Then, when I got back to my seat, I got talking to the local man, Ciaran. He was pretty drunk by the end of the evening. He said something interesting."

"Oh yes?" Dan was trying to concentrate, but he could already feel the beginnings of a headache making his skull feel like it was being slowly constricted in a vice.

"He said no more English would come to the island, but they had done once. He said Hugh was the only one left and that's because he was too broken to leave." Tyler yawned. "Only, I was intrigued by this, although I got the sense the landlord and Mick didn't want Ciaran to say any more. They kept changing the subject. Then, I thought about Ian Lester going to visit this old Hugh fella and I wondered if there was any kind of connection. Though I can't think what it could be." Tyler waited for his colleague to reply. Eventually, he shook Dan's leg, but received only an undignified snort as a response. The young officer rose to his feet and sighed, leaving his friend passed out cold on his bed.

Chapter 30

Charlie was playing happily on a soft rug in the centre of the living room floor. Sharon was cross-legged beside him, handing the toddler brightly coloured bricks which he was then adding to an unstable tower.

Alice sat on the sofa opposite, cradling a mug of tea. "I just can't be certain she was the same woman who I found leaning over Charlie in the car. The weather was terrible that afternoon and she had a hood over her hair, but she seemed so very familiar, when she stepped into that lift."

"She was wearing work clothes, so she must have a job in one of those business that share the building with Earth's Saviours. Which floor did she get into the lift from?"

"I think it was the third. It wouldn't be difficult to find out what business has offices there. But then, what would be my reason for enquiring? She's not a suspect in any crime. I'm not even sure it's the same woman."

"Well, we can find out plenty online, without having to use police channels." Sharon clapped as Charlie placed the final brick on the top. He mirrored her gesture, striking his two pudgy palms together with a dribbly grin.

Alice sighed, feeling suddenly exhausted. "I can't get side-tracked by this woman. The Lester case is too important."

"Have we heard anything from the officers who are on surveillance at Garscadden yet?"

"They've not spotted our suspect so far. But after what Macy McAdams said today, I reckon she won't have that bright red hair any longer. Beyond that, we don't have much of a description of her."

Sharon levered herself to her feet shakily, stretching out her cramped thighs, thinking that maybe she should take up yoga or something. "I think we should take another look at the list of volunteers who work at the Argyll Forest, speak to a few perhaps? I know there was no Billi Star on the list, but maybe she's helped out there from time to time. It's obvious she's an environmentalist of some kind, who moves from place to place."

Alice nodded. "Yeah, we might as well. What was the name of the manager there? It might be worth sending him the CCTV footage, see if he recognises her?"

"Todd McCleary. I've got his email address somewhere."

Charlie had got to his feet too, as unsteadily as Sharon. He turned and toddled over to the sofa, lifting his arms up to his mum. Alice scooped him into her lap and held his warm, compact body to her chest, breathing in his smell of milk and baby powder. "Let's do that, then. First thing tomorrow. But for now you should head home, Sharon. Take the evening off."

The DS wasn't going to argue.

*

The following morning, Dermot had arrived at his desk early. He wanted to go through every single case Klara Laska had identified through her search parameters. Klara was currently expanding the analysis to include cases lodged more than ten years ago, but something told the DI their perpetrator hadn't been operating for that long. He wasn't sure why, just a hunch based on the mistakes made during Lester's murder.

The analyst was right. Many of the cases flagged up by the software were stabbings which were connected to street crimes or gang disputes, nothing to do with their case. He lifted his takeout coffee to his lips and sipped, rubbing his tired eyes. At this stage in an investigation, if they hadn't got a major lead, the fatigue started to set in. He couldn't afford for this to happen.

Dermot placed his cup down carefully and picked up his mobile. Without thinking too hard about it, he located the number for his contact at the Highlands and Islands division and placed the call.

"Hi, DC Stone? It's DI Muir here, from Glasgow. Thanks so much for the files you sent me. They were very useful. Listen, I was wondering if you could do me one more favour? If it's not too much trouble, of course?"

Chapter 31

Tyler rubbed the grubby pane of his hotel room window with the sleeve of his hoodie. It seemed to him that the rain had finally stopped, although a gale was still blowing through the warped wooden frames.

He wondered if Dan would be wanting breakfast. The detective gave a tentative knock at his colleague's door as he passed, thinking if there was no reply, he'd let him sleep a while longer.

The handle turned and Dan stood in the doorway. His hair was damp from the shower and he wore the clean but wrinkled clothes Maggie Sinclair had washed for them the previous day. His skin had a sickly pallor. "Christ. I feel awful."

"I wasn't sure you'd be up yet."

"I took a couple of paracetamol I found in my washbag. Now I need some coffee."

Tyler smiled. "Not ready for the 'full Scottish', then?"

Dan's face crinkled in disgust. "Don't even talk about it."

"Luckily for you, I don't have a great appetite either this morning. Coffee and toast will be fine."

Dan grabbed his jacket. "Right, let's get going, shall we?"

*

After breakfast, the detectives made their way along the main street in St Martin to the police station. The rain had indeed stopped, but the wind was still battering the sail boats moored in the harbour, making them sway at extreme angles in relation to the stone quay.

The fresh air was helping Dan's hangover to pass; that along with the three cups of black coffee he'd just drunk. The detective was still cursing himself for getting dragged into the whisky drinking session that had evolved the previous evening. Thankfully, Tyler had kept a clear head.

Eddie and Tracey were both at their desks when the detectives arrived.

"Any news on the ferry service?" Tyler asked as soon as they'd wished one another a good morning.

Eddie frowned. "The wind is still up. Hopefully in the next couple of days we can get the boat out."

Tyler didn't try to hide his disappointment.

Dan pulled out a chair, determined to find out as much information as he could before the weather broke and they could leave. "We had a few drinks in the pub last night, got talking to some of the locals."

"Mick said you were in," Tracey commented amiably.

"It seems Ian hasn't left the island in more than a year, not on Lonny's boat, anyway. There was also an older chap in the bar called Ciaran? He seemed to have lived on the island a long time?"

"Ciaran Millar? Aye, he lives in one of the wee cottages by the harbour. He used to fish from his own boat, but I think he's too old for it now," Eddie replied.

"Only, he said something odd, about there being no English settlers here on North Dorga, although there had been once. It sounded as if something had happened to drive them away?"

Tyler continued, "aye, Ciaran said that 'old Hugh' was the only settler who'd stayed and that was because he was too broken to leave."

Eddie rubbed the dark stubble on his chin. "Well, I really don't know what Millar was talking about. It's true we don't attract the English buyers that they get on Mainland, or up on Shetland. These twin islands are just too remote and too exposed. We've never had much of a tourist industry to speak of. Hugh Turner is English. He lives up at the last cottage before the lighthouse. His wife died about five years back and he didn't take it well. He's not all that old, maybe late fifties? But Millar's right, he's given up on life, let the building fall into disrepair. It's a sad situation, but he's no' family to step in and help."

"Ian was dropping in on him the other day," Dan said.

"Aye, Ian and Stevie make sure Hugh's got the basics of heat and water. Maggie will send over a home cooked casserole every once in a while."

"That's very good of them, considering they've got such a busy farm to be running?"

"This is a small island, DC Clifton," Tracey snapped. "We help one another out here. There's no council services on Dorga like you'd get on Mainland. There's a small health clinic in St Martin, but nothing like 'meals on wheels'. If you've a neighbour in trouble, you sort it out yourself." The woman seemed annoyed by the topic of conversation. Her cheeks had flushed pink.

"I just thought it was unusual for a young man like Ian to be so altruistic." Dan wanted to add that he was surprised Ian cared so much for a local man the same age pretty much as his own father when he had little to do with his own family. It struck him as odd.

"Maybe folk here are just nicer than they are in Glasgow." Tracey delivered the words coldly and stalked off the office floor into a room out the back.

"I'm sorry about that," Eddie sighed. "Tracey can be quite sensitive about any criticism of the island. She was born here and there've been times when the local council has suggested re-locating all the inhabitants to Mainland where there are better facilities and infrastructure, or even to Wick or John O'Groats. But the locals always refuse. This is their home. The authorities from the mainland aren't always welcome here as a result."

"I can understand that," Dan said, although he still thought the woman detective's behaviour was strange.

"Look, if you're so interested, why don't I drive you out to Hugh's place today? The rain seems to be holding off and I should probably check on the guy anyway?"

Dan got to his feet. "Yeah, that would be great."

Chapter 32

Rainwater had flooded most of the fields and the burns were full of gushing, peaty water. But the leaden clouds had dispersed and the odd ray of November sunshine cast an occasional slash across the lush landscape.

The east road did indeed stop abruptly by a set of three stone cottages and about four hundred yards from a lighthouse painted a faded blue and white.

Eddie brought the truck to a halt. "The lighthouse hasn't been manned since the sixties, but the light itself is operated from Kirkwall. The rocks out at the point can be very nasty for a small boat."

Dan climbed down from the passenger seat. The wind flapped his waterproof jacket as soon as he was out of the shelter of the Toyota. He swiftly zipped it up to the neck. Tyler wrapped his arms around his lean body, shivering against the cold.

The cottage Eddie led them towards had clearly once been painted white. Now, the stonework was exposed beneath the chipped paintwork which had been tarnished a dull grey by the elements. The window frames were rotten and splintering in places, the glass foxed with age and practically opaque.

Eddie knocked loudly on the door, then peered into the front sitting room through panes so salt water stained they looked almost like a piece of artwork. The house was as quiet as the grave. "There's a key in the shed round the back. We may have to use that."

Dan thought how little security there was in this island community. Maggie was right when she said they needed to trust one another. He took a few steps back along the front path, staring up to the distant headland, where the sun was attempting to break through a cloud above the pinnacle of the lighthouse. He took a deep breath of the sea air, which tasted brackish on his tongue. Then he spotted a dark figure making its way towards the cottage along a path from the lighthouse.

As the figure got closer, Dan could see it was a man with a thin wisp of grey hair, hunch-shouldered in a large waxed jacket. His expression was steely.

Eddie turned to greet him as he approached. "Hugh! I came to check if you had any damage after the storm."

The older man brushed past them and turned the key in the lock of the crumbling front door. He said nothing, but left the door open, as if they were meant to follow.

Tyler wrinkled his nose at the smell of the property. The aroma was a mixture of damp, oil and what he suspected were rotten clothes, never quite getting a chance to fully dry.

Hugh had shrugged off his jacket and hung it on a hook in the hallway. He went straight to an open fireplace in the front room and began making a careful structure of logs and paper in the grate. "One of my fences came down, but that seems to be the worst of it."

Dan was surprised by how well-spoken the man was. "I'm DC Clifton and this is my colleague DC Sullivan from Glasgow. We were here on a police matter when the weather prevented us from returning to the mainland. For the time being, we are accompanying DC Shewan on his regular duties. We thought we could maybe have a chat about how things are going here?"

Hugh Turner stopped what he was doing and glared straight at the officers; a look of suspicion and what also appeared to be hostility in his green eyes. "You've no business to come here. What do you want?"

"Come now Hugh, like DC Clifton said, they're just tagging along wi' me. It's been useful to have an extra pair of hands to be honest, what with the storms an' everything. We just want to make sure you're okay out here."

The man struck a match and tossed it onto his untidy pyramid, watching as the flames curled the paper and licked at the edges of the logs. "The police have never been of any bloody use to me."

Eddie looked affronted. "I've done my best Hugh. But you really need some proper work done on this place. I can't see it lasting another winter otherwise."

Hugh stared at the fire. "I didn't mean that. You've been a good friend to me, Eddie. I wish you'd been in the job when it really mattered. But it's too late now."

Dan bent down so he was level with the man. "What do you mean Mr Turner? When *did* it matter?"

He whipped his head round, his eyes reflecting the flames, burning with hate. "Get out of my house!" he hissed. "Haven't you people done enough? Leave me alone, I tell you!"

Eddie shook his head sadly. "Come on, we'd better leave."

Dan and Tyler followed the other detective outside, pulling the door shut behind them. As they walked in silence back to the truck, the wind howled around the lighthouse, as if in agreement that they were not welcome here.

Chapter 33

Dusk had fallen by four pm. It would be dark soon. Although, the lights on this street were particularly efficient, the woman had noticed. She needed to make sure she avoided standing beneath one in order not to be seen.

The first wave of folk were arriving home; those who picked their children up from school or nursery. The second wave would come later, when the full-time workers returned; those who were at their desks well into the evening, or visited pubs or made shopping trips on their way. People like herself.

The policewoman had been at home for half an hour. She brought her little boy into the house when there was still a shimmer of lingering daylight. She hadn't left him sitting in the car seat again, but carried him awkwardly on her hip as she fumbled for her key.

There had been about ten minutes when the living room curtains remained open. She could see the boy sitting on a rug, surrounded by his toys, sipping a cup of juice contentedly. Then the policewoman with the auburn hair pulled the thick drapes closed and her window on their lives was shut.

She stood on the corner a little while longer. Other houses on this street had their lights blazing and never bothered with curtains at all. She could observe most of their evening rituals if she wanted to; the dogs running in circles of excitement at the return of their owners, the TV dinners and the piano practice.

But she wasn't terribly interested in them, although she had watched such families in the past. Or even in the husband with the dark wavy hair and tailored suits. He would be back in an hour or so, but she wouldn't wait. Her feet were beginning to feel numb in her court shoes, her tights were only fifteen denier. She hated the thick ones, which bunched around the ankles. She liked to be smart for work, even if it meant braving the chill at this time of year. She pulled the hood up on her dark coat and continued walking, smiling to herself, knowing she'd be back in plenty of time for the evening news.

*

Dermot had joined Klara at her temporary workstation. He'd brought the analyst in a cup of takeout mint tea, from the coffee bar on the corner, knowing this was her preferred beverage and aware that he'd probably trespassed on her remit with the work he'd been doing himself in the last day. Deciding he might need a peace offering.

She sipped the aromatic drink whilst sifting through the lines of data she'd generated on her screen. "I haven't got anything new for you yet, DI Muir."

"No, I'm not chasing you for results." He cleared his throat. "The DCI and myself took a particular interest in the Mabel Flett case you showed us. There was something about the dressing of the murder scene which made us curious. I requested the full file from the investigating department."

Klara took off her glasses and gave him her full attention. Her eyes were a sea-green, flecked with amber. "Did you find anything of interest?"

"We are pretty sure the teddy bear found at the scene in Caithness was placed there *after* the murder, by the killer themselves. In fact, I took the liberty of contacting Highlands and Islands again, to ask about other unsolved crimes within their division. I didn't ask them to apply any of our criteria, I just wanted to see what they came up with."

"Do you think that specific region has a connection to the Lester murder?" She looked sceptical.

Dermot shrugged. "It's just a hunch. Wick can't be more than a few miles from North Dorga, the place DCs Clifton and Sullivan have visited to speak with Lester's son, even if there is a strip of North Sea between them. I don't think it's something we can afford to ignore."

Klara pursed her lips. "An analyst's work is only as good as the information we have been given to set our research parameters. If we miss out a key criteria, it's possible to overlook a valuable piece of information. My work isn't infallible. What did they send you?"

Dermot was relieved he hadn't offended her. "Great. I'll send you over the details of a case that jumped out at me. I'd appreciate your input before I take it to Bevan?"

Klara slipped her glasses back on and smiled. "Of course, and thank you for the tea."

Dermot was making his way back to his own desk when Sharon cut across the office floor to intercept him. "Have you got a minute? There's something I'd like you to see?"

Why he felt a flash of irritation at Sharon's request he really didn't know. It was hardly justified. "Sure."

Sharon led him to her untidy desk, a notebook scrawled with text lay open beside her computer screen. Alice was seated opposite, also leaning forward with an interested expression.

The DS continued. "We are of course still trying to track down the whereabouts of Elinor Lester, AKA Billi Star, but at the same time I've been doing some research into the cross symbols used at both Lester's crime scene and that of Mabel Flett."

Dermot felt a tingling sensation in his chest that felt almost like excitement. He wondered if Sharon had found something important here. She had great instincts.

Sharon pointed at the screen. "I was surfing the internet, trying to find out whatever I could about 'palm crosses'. I already know pretty much everything about the wooden crosses used by Earth's Saviours. Only, I found this website fairly quickly and it came as something of a surprise."

Dermot scanned the text, his eyebrows rising.

Sharon addressed Alice. "You see, it seems as if our Easter 'palm crosses' are also known as 'African palms'. In fact, although now widely copied, they started out as quite a localised piece of craftwork, made only in eight villages in the Masasi area of southern Tanzania."

Alice gasped. "Where Quentin Lester worked for six years?"

"Yep," Sharon replied.

"I don't know what the hell this means," Dermot said excitedly. "But it provides another link between the murders of Quentin Lester and Mabel Flett." He grinned. "Sharon, I could kiss you!"

The DS shrugged off the praise, her face reddening to a deep crimson.

Chapter 34

Sharon searched for the sunglasses she'd tossed into her bag the previous night, at her flat in Glasgow. The sun was hanging low over the lush Simba hill, the outcrop of rock and soil that dominated the city of Dodoma, but it remained brighter than anything she'd experienced before. The heat was expected, but the DS still felt the sweat prickling the back of her neck beneath the collar of the lemon yellow cotton shirt she was wearing.

Dermot seemed unaffected by the change in climate. His light suit was uncreased and crisp, even after the long flight. He led the way out of the airport and headed straight for one of the waiting taxi cabs. Allowing the driver to lift their small cases into the boot.

The air-conditioning in the back of the car was a welcome relief. "I still can't quite believe the DCS allowed us to come."

Dermot twisted the lid on a bottle of water and took a gulp. "He's got a huge budget allocated to him by the First Minister. We need to get this murder solved so that it doesn't forever taint Scotland's hosting of COP26. If we can't be seen to keep delegates safe, then Glasgow won't be chosen for any high-level conferences ever again."

Sharon wasn't sure this was such a bad thing. The entire city had been brought to a halt and her fellow officers placed under unbelievable pressure. But she knew Dermot had greater sympathy with the establishment powers than her so didn't comment on it. "It's a shame Alice couldn't come too."

"Yes, this is her lead as much as yours. But she couldn't leave Charlie, I totally understand." He gave a wistful smile. "Whereas you and I..."

Sharon nodded. He didn't have to say any more. She and Dermot were single and without ties. Not even a pet between them. They could jet off to another continent with just a few hours' notice. "Yeah, I take your point. Like Dan and Tyler; single and carefree. God, I hope we don't get stranded here like they have on Dorga."

Dermot chuckled. "We couldn't be in more different places. We're hardly going to experience a winter storm here." He glanced out of the window at the landscape which was interspersed with greenery but mostly populated by parched fields and low-rise stone dwellings.

"I wonder if that's why Lester chose to come here? Because it's so much different from Scotland?"

"Maybe he just wanted to do good? Tanzania is one of the poorest countries in Africa?"

Sharon thought it could be a bit of both.

It took thirty minutes for them to reach the cream stone building that housed Simon Clarke's charity. Dermot paid the driver, who had left their cases standing solitary in the dust.

A tall white man with a deeply tanned face emerged from the front of the building. He held out his hand to the detectives. "I'm Simon. You are very welcome to our headquarters here at 'Teaching Tanzania'.

Sharon placed him in his early fifties. "Thanks so much for agreeing to see us at such short notice."

He led them inside the building which was pleasantly cool. A shaded corridor led to an open-air quad with a raised flower-bed in the centre, filled with African violets and Lobelia. Just off this courtyard was an office that housed three desks. "Take a seat, please. Would you like a drink?"

Dermot shook his head. "We've had plenty of water, thanks."

"Is this your first time in Africa?" The man asked with a wide smile.

"Yes," Sharon said. "It is for me. What a wonderful city this is."

Simon nodded enthusiastically. "I've lived here now for fifteen years. I divide my time between Dodoma and the villages where we have established our schools. It is a remarkable place. If you do have the time, we have elephants, lions and hippos to be seen in their natural habitats. You must take one of the safari tours in the Northern Masailand, they are quite famous."

"We won't have time for that," Dermot interrupted. "We are here to find out about Quentin Lester."

Simon's face became serious. "Of course, although, as I told you on the phone, he was a quiet member of the team. I didn't feel I got to know him particularly well, but he was a hard worker. He was good at raising funds for our projects and wasn't afraid to get his hands dirty."

"Did he talk about his family much?"

Simon frowned in thought. "I believe he mentioned his son a few times, especially when we were based out in the villages. He said he'd started work on a farm on one of the Scottish islands. I sensed he was quite proud of him."

"He never mentioned his daughter?" Sharon probed.

"No, I don't think so. But you can speak with other members of my team. They may have known him better."

"We will, thank you."

Sharon removed some printed sheets from her bag and placed them on the table. "This may sound like a strange question, but do you know anything about the palm crosses that are made in the Masasi region? I believe a number of your schools are in that area?"

Simon took the sheets with interest, they described the process and sale of the crosses. "We don't sell the crosses ourselves, but a few of our fellow charities do. There was a British Anglican missionary in the 1960s who founded the charity that sell the African palm crosses. He felt that the traditional, handmade symbols would be well received back in the UK and America, particularly for the Palm Sunday celebrations. He was right. The local farming families still produce them. The proceeds go straight back to the local communities. It was seen as a way of encouraging the farmers to help themselves. Although, it was also a means of spreading Christianity to these communities." Simon crossed his arms over his chest. "*We* are a non-religious charity. We aim to spread education, not doctrine."

"But these crosses are still produced?"

"Oh yes, and they sell very well around the world. The project has been extremely successful."

"What about Quentin? Would he have had anything to do with the distribution of these crosses?"

"Absolutely not. He worked solely for our charity. But whether he bought any for himself, I've no idea. We often passed through the villages known for the craft, he could easily have picked some up, but I don't recall it. I don't remember him being a particularly religious man either, so it wouldn't make much sense for him to have one."

Sharon felt her heart sink. Had they travelled all this way for nothing? Had her research sent them on an expensive wild goose chase?

Dermot seemed unperturbed. "It's getting late. Thank you for seeing us today, at such short notice, but it's time for us to head to our hotel. Is it still alright for us to return in the morning and question some of your employees?"

Simon held out his arms in an expansive gesture. "Of course. I'd love to introduce you to my team. I can show you the plans for the many projects we have completed since we began the charity. We are very proud of them."

Dermot nodded. He was grateful for the man's openness and cooperation, but he couldn't help feeling there was something he wasn't telling them. It felt like they were being given the slick sales pitch that Simon Clarke had perfected on potential donors over the years. But he and Sharon needed to dig beneath the marketing spiel; find out what it was really like to live and work out here in this land so different to their own.

Chapter 35

Klara approached the DCI's office and gave a tentative knock. She saw the senior detective raise her head from her paperwork and beckon her in.

"What can I help you with?" Dani asked.

"Well, since DI Muir left in such a hurry, I wasn't sure who to report to with these case notes he left me?"

Dani felt a surge of frustration. The analyst could surely have approached Alice or another member of the team? But she swallowed down this retort. "Okay, what did Dermot have you working on?"

Klara explained how Dermot had requested the details of all serious criminal investigations in the Highlands and Islands region in the last few years from his contact up there. He'd wanted her to examine the details of a specific case he'd highlighted, before taking it to the DCI herself.

Dani sat up straighter in her seat, becoming more interested in what the analyst had to say. "Have you got the file there?"

"Yes, I wanted to pass it onto you, as that was what DI Muir was intending. I think the trip to Africa would have made it slip from his mind."

"Take a seat, Klara. Why don't you explain the details for me?"

The woman pulled up a chair and perched on the edge. "The murder of Mabel Flett took place in April 2017. DI Muir had also obtained the file on a case of death by dangerous driving which occurred a few months before, in Westhill, Inverness."

Dani furrowed her brow. She couldn't see how looking at a fatal traffic accident from five years before was going to take their case any further forward.

Klara seemed to sense her scepticism. "Yes, I thought the details appeared entirely unrelated too, until I examined them more closely. Perhaps I should explain? It was early February 2017 and a woman named Irene Vickers left her house on a modern estate in Westhill to walk to work along the Culloden Road, as she usually did. She was the manager of a nursery school a couple of miles from her home. Her husband confirmed she left the house at 8.30am."

"Witnesses reported the road was busy with traffic, as it usually was in the mornings. At 8.50am the local police received a 999 call. A white van belonging to a local furniture warehouse was flagged down at a traffic light interchange, some pedestrians had been trying to gain the driver's attention from the pavement for some metres before it finally stopped at a red light."

Dani shook her head to indicate confusion.

Klara continued, "witnesses had noticed what they at first thought was a grey bundle attached to the back bumper of the van as it drove past. Then, a couple of them realised to their horror, it was actually a person, being dragged behind the vehicle, caught somehow on the fender."

Dani's face drained of colour. "Was it Irene Vickers?"

Klara nodded. "At the traffic lights, someone banged on the driver's window and he finally stopped. The police and an ambulance were called. Irene's grey coat had somehow got wrapped around the rear bumper of the van. She must have tried to free herself, but then the vehicle started moving." She cleared her throat. "The woman died from her injuries at the scene, which were consistent with being dragged along tarmac at thirty to forty miles an hour for a distance of roughly one and a half miles. She was 59 years old."

"Christ! Did the driver of the van have no idea she was there?"

"No, he claims not. There was some CCTV footage, showing Mrs Vickers being dragged by the vehicle, but none indicating how she got attached to it in the first place."

"What did the police conclude?"

"The investigating officer suggested Mrs Vickers may have attempted to cross the road behind the vehicle and stumbled, finding herself entangled by her coat in the bumper of the van. It pulled away before she had a chance to free herself. The driver was found to have been speeding along this stretch of the road and he'd failed to respond to several pedestrians who had attempted to flag him down."

"Hence the dangerous driving charge."

"The driver was sentenced to two years for causing death by dangerous driving and lost his licence. I know it doesn't sound like much, but in court he stressed he had no idea the woman was being dragged by his vehicle. He showed great remorse."

"There's never a long custodial sentence for driving offences, even when people are killed," Dani said absent-mindedly. "I know it was a bizarre and gruesome case, but why did Dermot single it out for me to look at?"

"He didn't get a chance to say, but I think it might have been this," Klara opened the file and retrieved several of the crime scene photos, sliding them across the desk towards the DCI.

Dani took one and examined it closely. The glossy print was of the rear of the white van, covered in a veneer of dirt. Poor Irene Vickers had mercifully been removed from the rear bumper, but her grey coat was still entangled in its rusting metal. But beside the coat, squeezed between the bumper and the rear lights, was a small brown teddy bear, sporting a red ribbon around its neck. Dani dropped the photograph as if it had scalded her hands. "Where had the teddy come from? Was it on the vehicle before the accident?"

Klara shook her head. "DI Muir had phoned the investigating officer to ask. He'd added the notes to the file. The driver claimed he didn't recognise it, although he said he had placed mascots on his vans in the past. Nobody took much notice of its presence as far as I can tell. It didn't seem important in the face of such a tragic death."

"No, I suppose it wouldn't have."

"Was I right to bring this case to your attention, DCI Bevan?"

Dani's mind was ticking over. "Yes, Klara. You were absolutely right."

Chapter 36

The hotel room was basic. There was an en-suite bathroom with a shower connected to a bath with chipped enamel, but the water was a lukewarm drizzle. Sharon had barely managed to rinse the shampoo out of her curly hair.

Towelling herself dry, Sharon was resigned to allowing her hair to form a tight, dry frizz in the heat and humidity. What did it matter? They were there to do a job.

Dermot had already arrived at the breakfast room when she came downstairs. He was piling a plate with chopped fruit. Sharon joined him and did the same, filling a China cup from the cafetière resting on its hotplate. They took a table by the double-doors looking out onto an arid garden area with palms planted in large terracotta pots.

"We've got permission to question Simon's staff today," Dermot commented, gulping down a mouthful of coffee.

Sharon sighed. "Now we're here in Tanzania, it feels as if the use of the African cross, in a murder not even directly related to that of Quentin Lester, was a tenuous reason to come. It may just be a coincidence after all."

"Regardless of the importance of the cross, I'm keen to find out more about Lester's life here. I feel like Simon Clarke is a bit too slick, do you know what I mean? These ex-pats, living out here without family or friends, they must get close to their workmates, mustn't they? Lester couldn't possibly have lived here for all those years without leaving a mark?"

Sharon sipped her coffee in silence. She couldn't help but agree. Here was a man who had fallen out with every member of his family, had generated enough hatred in another human being for them to drive a stake into his chest. He'd done something to upset people, that was for sure.

Dermot pushed his empty plate to the side, pulling on his linen jacket. "Come on, let's go and find out."

*

The heat was intensifying as the morning wore on. Sharon was grateful for the shaded stone building that housed the 'Teaching Tanzania' charity offices. She couldn't imagine what it would be like outside in the direct sunlight.

They were questioning a woman named Marie, who was one of the staff who originated from Tanzania. She had only been working for the charity for a couple of years and hadn't known Quentin Lester at all. Dermot wiped sweat from his brow, feeling this was a futile exercise if they weren't going to be allowed to speak with anyone who Quentin actually worked with.

Marie left them and retreated down a dark corridor. Dermot shook his head in frustration. "We need to speak to more people," he said.

Sharon rose from the desk they'd been allocated and began to explore the single-storey building. There was an open-plan conference room further along the corridor which was currently empty, but with evidence of a recent meeting in the form of scribbled notes on a flipchart in the corner.

The next room held a couple more desks and some filing cabinets. A lady in her fifties sat behind one of them, staring intently at a computer screen. Sharon brushed her knuckles against the door, gently clearing her throat. The woman looked up.

"I'm DS Sharon Moffett, from the Scottish police

service. I wondered if I might have a word with you?"

The woman's jet black hair was interspersed with streaks of pure white. She removed a pair of blue rimmed glasses and eyed the detective carefully. "Of course, do take a seat. I'm Rehema Omari. I thought Simon had devised an itinerary for you and the DI?"

"Yes, we've interviewed several members of staff already, but none of them really seemed to know Mr Lester. I'm afraid it's becoming a waste of our time."

Rehema sat back in her chair. "What is it you want to know? I worked with Quentin for all the years he was here in Tanzania."

Sharon pulled up a seat. "What did Quentin actually do for your charity?"

Rehema thought about this. "He was a fundraiser first and foremost. He travelled to nearby cities and lobbied companies for donations to our projects. He spent a lot of time in Dar es Salaam and here in Dodoma. He would present our projects to local businesspeople who wished to see Tanzania prosper and to lift the people out of poverty. Education is the key to that."

"And Lester was successful in that role?"

"Oh yes, he brought in many thousand US dollars to the charity. We built several schools during his time with us. Since he left, we haven't been quite as successful at raising funds. This is partly to do with the effects of the pandemic. Companies are nervous about investing their money."

"What about on a personal level? Were you friends with Lester?"

Rehema gave a wry smile. "We worked well on a professional level. Quentin was very driven to ensure our projects were successful. He had a genuine belief that education was the key to generating opportunities for the children of our poorest regions.

But as a man, I found him dull and pompous. He did not socialise with the rest of the team and seemed uninterested in getting to know our culture. He often made me think of the colonial missionaries, you know? Who are coming to the 'dark continent' to reform it, not to appreciate what is already here."

Sharon nodded, she could see exactly what the woman meant. "So why did he leave? He'd been here for six years and he wasn't many years away from retirement? Why go back to Scotland when he'd been so successful in this role?"

A shadow seemed to pass across the woman's eyes, as if a part of her had closed off. "Our colleagues from overseas never stay here forever, detective. They all return home in the end. It was the same for Quentin. They are here to do their good deeds and then they go back to the life they know."

Sharon thanked the woman for her time, but left the room with a sense that despite the praise she gave to his work here, Rehema Omari hadn't actually liked Quentin Lester at all.

Chapter 37

"It feels like we're finally getting somewhere." Dermot was drinking a gin and tonic in the hotel's bar. "From what she said, it sounds as if Rehema Omari didn't like Quentin one bit, which is not what Simon Clarke's been telling us. According to him, Quentin did amazing work and had almost no personality at all. His colleagues were entirely neutral towards him."

Sharon was nursing a glass of coke, for some reason wanting to keep her wits about her tonight. "Yes, but it doesn't exactly provide a motive for his murder, does it? Rehema thought the man was pompous and probably a bit superior about western culture, but she wasn't the one who killed him, was she?"

"No, but it means he wasn't quite as bland in his work life as we've been led to believe."

Sharon stirred the ice around the glass with her straw. "Yes, I definitely sensed that there was something else Rehema was holding back. I reckon Quentin Lester did something she wasn't happy about, but she wasn't going to tell me what it was."

"Something that reflected badly on the charity?"

"It must be. Perhaps Simon knows about it too? That's why he's not really allowed us to speak to anyone who actually knew Lester."

Dermot sighed, finishing the last of his G & T and signalling to the barman he wanted another. "It feels like we're being led down a cul-de-sac here at the charity headquarters. I did try to find out where Lester lived whilst he was here, but it seemed he moved from place to place, renting short-term or staying in hotel rooms. He certainly didn't put down roots in the country."

"Which is exactly what Rehema suggested."

"Do you want another drink?" Dermot raised his eyebrow.

"No thanks, I'll stick with this one."

"That's not like you? I thought you'd be trying out some of the local cocktails, so you could report back to Andy on the specialities of the region?"

"We aren't the department clowns, you know. Andy and I."

Dermot put down his drink in surprise. "Yes, of course. You're both brilliant detectives, I know that. But you don't take police life too seriously, that's all."

Sharon thought about this. "Actually, we do take it seriously, Andy probably more than most. It's because we know it's so important that we have to lighten the mood sometimes and spread a bit of comfort with the occasional treat. It doesn't mean we are figures of fun."

Dermot shook his head. "I wasn't saying that. It was just a throwaway remark, nothing more."

Sharon had lowered her eyes, for some reason not wanting to meet his gaze. She saw herself reflected back in the glass of her drink; her hair a frizzy halo around her head and her fair skin already turning a salmon pink on the cheeks and nose from the merciless sun. She took a deep breath and raised her head to face him. "I don't think we're getting anywhere here in Dodoma. I want to visit one of these schools that Quentin Lester helped to build. I think we should get Simon to ask one of his staff members to escort us to the south west of the country, where the majority of the 'Teaching Tanzania' projects are and where these African palms are actually made."

Dermot nodded, suddenly feeling he didn't really

want that second drink. “Yes, I think you’re right. I’ll call him on his mobile straightaway.” He pushed back his chair to go and make the call, momentarily keeping his eyes fixed on his colleague opposite, who he was beginning to see in a whole new way.

Chapter 38

Alice had developed an odd feeling. It had manifested itself since she'd seen that woman getting into the lift with her and Sharon. It was an overwhelming sensation that she was being watched.

She was a police officer, so it should have been easy enough to prove if this feeling was justified. Indeed, Alice had taken to getting up in the middle of the night to look out of the window of the bedroom she shared with Fergus to scan the street below, allowing her eyes to linger on all its shadowy corners. She was now also in the habit of glancing behind her at regular intervals as she walked Charlie from the car to nursery, but hadn't noticed anything suspicious to substantiate her fear.

It was only in the department that she felt totally safe. On the desk in front of her was a list of all the employees of the solicitor's firm based on the third floor of the building where Earth's Saviours had their offices in the vast loft space. The employees had been listed on their website. One of the names of the women on that inventory must have been the person they'd seen in the lift that day. But without making a formal request for personnel files, it would be difficult to find out which one it was.

Alice shoved the list back into the plain file she'd selected for it. Sharon and Dermot were in Africa, chasing up an important lead. Lester's daughter still remained untraced. She couldn't waste police time on what could well just be her own paranoia.

The DCs who had been on surveillance at Garscadden Station had been called back in. There had been no further sightings of Billi Star. Alice assumed her striking red hair would be a different colour by now. The DCI had briefed her on the death by dangerous driving case in Inverness that had featured the teddy bear with a red bow, just like the one placed at the scene of Mabel Flett's murder. Alice was intrigued by the parallel but didn't see what bearing it really had on their investigation. Klara Laska had been asked to look into those cases further, to dig into the backgrounds of the two women to see if they were connected in any way. These leads were all being investigated by her fellow officers.

Alice drummed her fingers on the desk before reaching over to Sharon's side to retrieve the pile of notes tottering there, abandoned when she'd had to leave in such a hurry. On the top, were the contact details for the manager of the information centre at the Argyll Forest. She picked up her extension and punched in the numbers written there.

"Hello, Woodland Scotland, Argyll Forest. How may I help?"

"Hello, is that Mr McCleary? It's DI Alice Mann here, I visited you with my colleague last week?"

"Yes, I remember. What can I do for you?"

"We had requested a list of your volunteers which you kindly supplied for us, but we are now looking for one specific individual who may have done some voluntary work for you. She goes under the name, Billi Star, although her birth name was Elinor Lester. Recently, she has worn her hair in a short, pixie cut and dyed a bright red, but it could have been any colour really, in the past. I've got a CCTV still of her, but it isn't actually very clear."

The line was silent for a few moments.

"Mr McCleary? Are you still there?"

"Yes, detective inspector. I assume these names were not on the list I gave you?"

"No, but I thought maybe there were other, more casual helpers in the forest from time to time?"

The man's tone became cold and distant. "We don't have *casual* labour here. In order to volunteer for Woodland Scotland, there are forms to be completed and a criminal database check to be undergone, as you must be well aware."

Alice felt like this conversation was getting her nowhere. "Okay, Mr McCleary, thanks for your time."

"Wait a second."

Alice felt a flicker of optimism bloom in her chest.

"You spoke with the wood carvers the last time you visited, yes?"

"That's correct."

"Well, although I don't encourage it, those lads do have some 'hangers-on' who can be found floating around the hut they use; smoking and lighting fires. There are often a few young ladies amongst them. In fact, Harry has headed into the city today to meet his sister, he was telling me. I can give you his mobile number. Perhaps you could ask him your questions whilst he's there?"

A broad smile formed on Alice's face. "Great idea. If you could give me that number, I'd be most grateful."

*

They met in a café opposite the imposing gothic frontage of the Cathedral, a few streets from the Earth's Saviours headquarters. Alice had bought a couple of coffees, setting them down on the Formica table.

Harry reached for his and swiftly added the contents of a sugar packet. "Cheers. I need this. It's a long drive down from the forest."

"Are you in town to deliver more crosses to your sister, for the Earth's Saviours demonstrations? Mr McCleary didn't mention it, but then I remembered you hadn't told him about your connection?"

"Oh aye, my sis says they've never been so busy what with the conference and everything. They've new members wanting to join all the time." He stirred his drink with a plastic spoon. "Although-" His young face creased into a frown.

"Although, what?"

"I handed over the crosses I'd made, very carefully carved they are, and I couldn't help but notice there were a bunch of volunteers stapling together their own versions of ma' crosses, only with cheap pieces of plywood."

"Ah," Alice blew on her cappuccino, "yes, I noticed how many reproductions of the crosses there are now. I suppose they need quantity rather than quality with all the demonstrations going on?"

He sighed. "Aye, I can appreciate that. But the whole point of the movement is that we want a world that embraces sustainable living and a resurrection of ancient skills. Not encouraging followers to attach reconstituted wood pulp with polymer glue."

Alice could very much see his point. It was important to reach new members as a pressure group but also inevitable your message may become diluted in the process. Interesting as the issue was, it wasn't why she was there. "Todd McCleary told me that you have some friends who hang around the hut with you, back at the forest. Only, there's a woman I'm trying to track down. She calls herself Billi Star although she was born Elinor Lester."

Alice was about to bring out the CCTV still from her bag when Harry replied, "aye, Billi visits the forest quite a lot, but mostly in summer. She and a few others bring their tents and stay for a while. They help us collect wood."

Alice felt her heart begin to pump hard in her chest. "This woman is in her early thirties and is currently wearing her hair in a short pixie cut, dyed red?”

“Yep, that sounds like her. Although, sometimes her hair is purple. She’s cool and a very good singer. Justin plays the guitar and they often do a set together, on summer evenings.” The man looked wistful.

Alice was clutching her cup so hard the hot water was beginning to scald her skin. “I don’t suppose you have an address for Billi? Or a way we might get in contact?”

He gave a chuckle. “Billi doesn’t have an address, she comes and goes. In summer, they camp in various places and in winter she’s got a few mates that let her bed down on their sofa. But she still lives in the 21st Century. I’ve got her number on my contacts list. She usually gives me a buzz when they’re planning on coming down to the forest.”

Alice kept her expression blank. “Listen, Harry. I’d really appreciate it if you could help me with something.”

Chapter 39

This version of Africa was the one Sharon had formed in her mind before they had arrived on the continent. She and Dermot had managed to persuade Simon Clarke to allow them to accompany one of his employees on a trip to the site of a new school being built in the southern Masasi region.

They had stopped in Dar es Salaam for the night and the journey had taken two days; along busy highways and then dusty tracks that shook the jeep so badly Sharon's bones were still aching. But the scene that greeted them in Ntwara was worth the discomfort.

The village consisted of three rows of circular huts, topped with thatched roofs and set amongst a landscape of low-lying, arid hills. The ground was covered in a yellowy sand. Children played football in a clearing bathed in the orange glow of the late afternoon sun, kicking up dust that resembled powdered gold.

Matthew, their escort from 'Teaching Tanzania', led the detectives towards a pre-fab on the edge of the village, overlooking the foundations of what would become the new school. "We started building last month when fresh funds came in from an international company. The structure should be completed in a couple of months. A local contractor is doing the work."

"How soon before the children can attend the school?" Sharon asked.

"We hope to begin to enrol early in the new year. Even without the building, our volunteers can still hold classes with the children and get them used to the learning process." Matthew opened the door of the pre-fab office and led them inside. Desks were pushed up to the windows and piles of paperwork spilled over their surfaces.

It was scorching hot. Sharon felt the sweat soaking the back of her shirt. “There’s quite a big difference between the cities and the villages, like these.”

Matthew nodded. “That’s why we are doing this job. It’s the more remote villages where access to education is required. There are schools in the larger cities, even in the slums. But out here, many of the farming families have no access to the education we take for granted.”

“Did Quentin Lester ever come out here, to this particular region?” Dermot asked.

“Oh yes, Quentin helped to build the school in the village five kilometres south of this one. I’ll take you there tomorrow. It’s one of our greatest successes. You will see how happy the children are.”

Sharon was desperate to step outside of the steel box the man used as an office. “Where will we sleep tonight?”

He pointed out of the window towards the far side of the village. “We have some large tents set up for our volunteers. I’m afraid that is where you will have to stay tonight. There are no hotels nearby without travelling a few hundred kilometres more.”

“That’s fine,” Sharon added. “We will make do, thanks.” She was actually quite relieved at the thought of sleeping under canvas, where they would surely feel the air cool as the sun finally set.

*

The tent comprised a circular wooden structure draped with a dusty orange coloured tarpaulin. A thin groundsheet covered the desert floor and Matthew had laid out a couple of roll mats and sleeping bags for the detectives.

Sharon was exhausted after the long journey in the relentless heat. She washed her face in a chipped pottery bowl and lay down on the makeshift bed. As darkness fell, the sounds of the African bush seemed to become amplified. Unidentified shrieks and the interminable rattle of the cicadas and frogs made her sit up with alarm, but gradually she got used to the ensemble of animal noises, eventually revelling in the sense it gave or being somewhere so very far removed from home.

Dermot entered the tent when it was pitch dark outside. He removed his jacket and trousers to a pair of tight boxer shorts and slid into his sleeping bag.

"What were you doing?" Sharon asked in a whisper.

Dermot started. "Sorry, I thought you were asleep. I was talking to Matthew by the camp fire. He offered me a glass of whisky. He said it would help me to sleep as the noises of the bush would be unfamiliar at first."

"Yes, they make quite a racket these animals. It's louder than the noise of the M8 from my flat window."

Dermot chuckled. "It's quite magical, though. Don't you think? Matthew pointed out the sound of a hippo, grunting in the distance somewhere."

Sharon levered herself up onto an elbow, she could just about see the silhouette of her companion in the gloom. "Have you been to Africa before?"

"I came on holiday with my parents and sister to Cape Town once. But we stayed in a hotel. It was nothing like this."

"I can see why the ex-pats working at the charity might fall in love with the place. But to stay forever? I don't know. I can understand why Quentin Lester returned in the end."

Dermot shifted round. "I don't know if it was

entirely his choice. From what Matthew was telling me this evening, Quentin fell out of favour with the charity managers, something about his methods not being compatible with the way the charity was moving forwards."

"Sounds like management speak."

Dermot sighed. "Yep, totally. I wish someone would give us a straight answer."

"Well, when we visit the school tomorrow, we may get a better idea." Sharon rested her head on the cushion she'd been given, closing her eyes and allowing the hum of the nocturnal creatures of the Masasi to lull her to sleep.

Chapter 40

When Sharon opened her eyes, she saw the entrance to the tent was unzipped. The sleeping bag beside her was empty. She got to her feet stiffly, feeling the effects of sleeping pretty much on the hard ground.

She pulled on her cotton trousers and splashed her face with water from the bowl, now tepid in the growing heat.

Outside the tent, the sun was rising steadily above the distant hills. The sky was a deep, lilac blue and Sharon had to squint against the brightness. She felt a headache beginning to build behind her eyes and suspected she wasn't drinking enough of the bottled water they'd brought with them.

Dermot was sitting on a camp chair drinking tea from a tin mug. He waved her over. "We're leaving in half an hour. Make sure you get some breakfast."

Matthew approached their little camp with a basket of mangoes. He took one out and laid it on the dusty ground, producing a long-bladed knife from his belt, he promptly chopped it in two. "Here, have this," he handed one half to Sharon.

"That's one hell of a knife you've got there. I don't believe it would be legal to carry in the UK," Sharon added warily.

"If you are travelling into the bush on your own, it's needed. Not least to cut fruit." He grinned.

Sharon bit into the sweet, watery fruit, wondering what else the knife might be needed for out here. In case a wild animal attacked, she supposed.

"I've added some more petrol to the jeep," Matthew continued. "We can continue on to Lomba village as soon as you're both ready."

Dermot drained his mug. "Just give us ten minutes, then we can head on our way."

*

The journey to Lomba took just under an hour. Beyond Ntwara, the road was no more than a dirt track. The suspension of the jeep wasn't enough to prevent Sharon's lower back jarring with every bump and jolt.

It was noon when they arrived in the village. It was larger than the one they'd just left. The villagers' huts were positioned around some Acacia trees and what appeared to be a water well. To the east of the village was a building that Sharon assumed was their new school. It was brick built and single storey, but had a sloping roof adorned with terracotta tiles that shone bright in the sun.

Matthew climbed down from the jeep and led them proudly towards the school. As they got closer, Sharon could see that a fence ran around the building. Within its grounds was a play area with a wooden climbing frame and hopscotch squares painted onto the concrete in primary colours.

"The children are still in class, but they will come out for their lunch break soon. Would you like to see inside?" Matthew punched a code into a panel on the gate in the fence and approached the entrance doors. The detectives gladly followed.

The building comprised two large classrooms and a couple of offices. Roughly forty children were divided between the two teaching rooms. They sat at old-fashioned flip-top desks and wore yellow t-shirts and grey shorts.

The teachers were addressing the students from the front of the class and the atmosphere was quiet and studious. Sharon was amazed to see what the charity had created here. She felt a lump forming in her throat at the idea these children may not have had a chance to attend school at all without the charity's intervention.

The sound of a buzzer filled the small building and the teachers dismissed their classes for lunch. Sharon and Dermot stood back and observed the students lining up in the corridor to receive a bowl of rice and vegetables from a lady in a white apron.

Matthew led them back outside. "You can see how well the children are doing here."

"Yes," Dermot agreed. "Are the children all from this village?"

"No, not all of them. We can cater for greater numbers than just the purely local children. In fact, we have a few more places in this school to fill yet." Matthew strode off ahead, towards another set of pre-fab buildings. These ones were filled with charity workers; conspicuous because of the 'Teaching Tanzania' t-shirts they wore. He pulled open the door of one. "Come out and meet our visitors! A couple of police detectives from Scotland."

A young man and woman climbed down the metal steps. "Hi! Welcome to Lomba!"

Sharon took the woman's outstretched hand. She was in her mid-twenties, of British origin. The detective thought she identified a Manchester accent.

The young man was also British, he was tall and lean and had the sort of plummy tones common to an English public school. "I'm Adam and this is Talia. We've been out here volunteering for just over a year, so we've seen the school rise up from the desert. Totally amazing!"

Dermot nodded. "The children certainly seem to be happy."

"Oh yes, great kids. We've been teaching them cricket and a bit of rugby, to boot!"

Sharon found this young man's enthusiasm grating. She turned to Matthew. "Are there any villages nearby where they produce the African palm crosses? I'm very interested to take one home with me, if I can?"

The man crinkled his tanned brow. "I'm not sure. Do you know, Adam?"

The younger man nodded enthusiastically. "Yeah, there's a farm a couple of kilometres out west where the family make them." He addressed Sharon. "The crosses get sold to a charity that then sells them on overseas. The farmers get a decent cut of the profits. It's a trade that's been flourishing for decades, but not something our organisation is involved with."

"Could you take me?" Sharon asked.

Matthew shrugged his shoulders, as if completely perplexed by the request. "Sure, if you want."

Adam stepped forward. "I'll drive the detective. I need to head out in that direction anyway, we've got some outreach workers in that region today. I can check on their progress while we're there."

"Ok, fine."

"I'll stay here and interview some of the staff at the school," Dermot added, not sure what his colleague was really hoping to achieve with this jaunt.

"Not a problem," Sharon replied. She nudged the young volunteer. "Come on, let's hit the road."

Chapter 41

Talia had lent Sharon a pair of sunglasses, she'd left her other pair in one of the hotel rooms they'd stayed in. She was grateful for them as the midday sun was reflected back off the parched ground and through the dirty windscreen.

Adam was driving faster than Matthew had. Sharon gripped the dashboard with both hands. They seemed to be heading deeper into the savannah. The occasional shrub or gnarled tree dotted the landscape, otherwise they were surrounded by a vast, arid plain.

Finally, when Sharon wasn't sure her body could take any more punishment from the uneven terrain, they saw the outline of a farm up ahead on the roadside. Another jeep was parked up on the shrubland beside one of the stone buildings.

"This is it," Adam declared, coming to an abrupt stop at the side of the track. "The family are called Hamisi; there are four kids. It's the mum who makes the crosses, she's very skilled at it."

Sharon climbed down from the jeep and looked around. The farm was a collection of stone buildings and wooden shacks. A field of goats was fenced off to the east of the building. Adam led them up to the entrance of the main house. He turned to his companion. "The family only speak Swahili I'm afraid. Some of our volunteers are fluent, but I'm not so good at the language yet."

The house seemed empty. Sharon was reluctant to enter without the owner's permission, but Adam pushed open the door, made of woven reeds, and proceeded down a dark corridor.

Sharon glanced into a side room, where she saw a blanket on the floor, filled with dried strips of palm leaf. She could see a pile of completed crosses in a basket to one side. She felt a sense of relief lighten the tightness in her chest. For what it was worth, she'd finally found what she'd come here to see.

The house seemed eerily quiet. Sharon touched Adam's arm. "Maybe they aren't here. We shouldn't trespass. I can leave some dollars and take one of the crosses. I'll be sure to leave a fair amount."

Adam shook his head. "The family are always around somewhere. There isn't anywhere else for them to go. Besides, some of our outreach staff are here, I saw their jeep outside."

Reluctantly, the detective followed. Adam walked confidently out of the rear of the house and into a sandy courtyard. The goats eyed them suspiciously from their pen. Sharon squinted into the sunshine. She could see a group of people a few metres up ahead. They seemed to be involved in some kind of altercation.

"What's going on?" Sharon asked warily.

"I don't know. That's Frank who's with them, he's one of our guys. We'd better go and check."

They walked beyond the courtyard and into a field filled with a low-lying, bushy crop of some kind, cultivated into rows creating a set of natural footpaths. As they grew closer to the group, Sharon could see a woman, who she assumed was Mrs Hamisi, holding onto a small boy, who was maybe seven or eight years old. Frank, wearing a 'Teaching Tanzania' t-shirt, damp with sweat, was remonstrating with her, whilst a couple of younger children clung to her legs, hiding their faces within the expansive cotton material of her skirt.

Abruptly, the man Adam said was Frank, reached forward and took the boy by the arm, physically dragging him away from his mother.

Instinctively, Sharon jogged up to the group. "Whoa, what's going on here? You can't manhandle that child." She glared at the charity worker.

He turned in her direction, a puzzled expression on his face. "But Mohammed Hamisi is enrolled in the school at Lomba. I've been sent to fetch him. He's nearly eight and needs to be in school." Frank looked over the detective's shoulder. "Adam, could you give me a hand here?"

Sharon took in the scene. "Where is Mr Hamisi?"

Frank shook his head in irritation. "He's out in the fields somewhere. That's why we have to take the boy now. His father doesn't really understand what we're trying to do here."

Sharon felt her cheeks flush with a growing anger. "You realise that Mohammed requires his parents' permission in order to attend your school. You can't just take him against his will?"

Adam stepped forward, dropping his voice. "We aren't in the UK now. We don't have to follow those kinds of rules."

"I'm sure there are laws in Tanzania against kidnapping," Sharon added coldly.

Frank dropped the boy's arm. "Come on, I'm not doing anything like that. If Mohammed stays here, he'll never learn to read and write. He'll be stuck on this farm forever. We want what's best for him."

Sharon looked at Mrs Hamisi. Her face was wet with tears, she was glancing rapidly between the detective and the man in the damp t-shirt, clearly not sure what was going on. Sharon walked slowly towards the family, her hands outstretched in what she hoped was a peaceful gesture. She stood between Frank and the mother and her children, suddenly realising how alone they were out here in the savannah. She didn't even know where the nearest police station was. "I know you don't understand what I'm saying, Mrs Hamisi, but I'm not going to let this man take your child. I'll wait until your husband returns from the fields if I have to."

The woman tipped her head to one side, pulling her eldest son back towards her, watching the detective with the frizz of blond hair and pink shiny skin intently.

Frank muttered an expletive. "For Christ's sake. I'm supposed to take Mohammed back with me today. What am I going to tell Matthew?"

Adam placed a hand on his arm. "You're supposed to persuade the family, Frank. Not drag the child off them. I thought you were meant to have an interpreter with you today?"

"She's sick. I just thought, he's missed so much school already, you know?" He glanced at his colleague imploringly.

"We need to go back to Lomba now Frank, and leave the Hamisi family alone."

Frank relaxed his stance begrudgingly.

Adam turned his head. "Come on detective, I'll drive all three of us back to the village. This has been a terrible misunderstanding, but we won't be taking Mohammed today."

When she was sure the two men were heading away from the farm, Sharon followed. She nodded to Mrs Hamisi as they left, but she was far too angry to be able to speak.

Chapter 42

Alice stood at the foot of the steps leading to the City Chambers in George Square. She pulled her black woollen coat more tightly around her as the chill began to bite. She glanced to her right, checking that Andy Calder was in position. She could see him loitering in front of one of the impressive lions on the cream stone cenotaph. Harry was standing with his hands shoved into his pockets on the other side of the monument, his head hanging down.

The DI scanned the entire square, knowing their quarry could approach from any direction. She checked her watch. It was almost midday.

Suddenly, a figure dressed in a denim jacket, with cropped hair the colour of palma violets, strode towards Harry's side of the cenotaph. Alice spoke quietly into her radio, ensuring Andy had also clocked the woman's approach.

Andy doubled-back and walked casually around to the north side of the monument. He stopped when he got close enough to see Harry approach the figure with the purple hair. Simultaneously, he and Alice closed in on the woman, spreading out their arms in order to minimise the chance of her bolting for a second time.

The woman gave the young man she was meeting a glare that flashed pure anger. "What's all this?" She demanded. "I thought this meeting was just you and me? That's what you said on the phone?"

Harry stepped forward. "The police were trying to get hold of you, Billi. There's news about your father that you need to hear. I didn't mean to trick you, but I thought it was important. There's no need to fear the police, they're on your side."

Billi Star gave her friend a withering stare, as if he were the stupidest person on the planet.

Alice hooked her arm through the woman's. "Do you confirm that you are Billi Star? Formerly, Elinor Lester?"

The woman nodded. "Yes, you obviously know that already."

"We need to take you in for questioning in relation to a very serious crime."

She shrugged. "Okay then, let's get this over with."

Alice glanced over her shoulder at Harry as they led the woman towards a squad car parked on a side street off the square. He was watching them depart, his shoulders hunched and looking like he might be about to cry.

*

Billi Star was seated in the interview room at Pitt Street opposite Alice and Andy. She had refused to have the duty solicitor accompany her. Alice had asked her to confirm her name for the digital recording.

"I'm Billi Star."

"And what is your current address?"

"I don't have one, I'm staying with a friend."

"In Glasgow?"

She sighed heavily. "Yes, in Scotstoun."

"Not far from Garscadden Station?"

"Aye. Were you one of the ones who chased me?" She made eye contact with Alice, her gaze was surprisingly penetrating.

"Yes. We only wanted to speak with you. To let you know the news about your father."

"That he's been murdered? Well, you've told me now, haven't you? So you can let me go again."

"You don't seem very surprised, about your father's violent death?" Andy leant forward, resting his elbows on the scratched table.

Billi laughed. "Haven't you discovered yet? My father wasn't a very nice man."

"We know you and your brother are estranged from him. Ian told us he was a strict parent who wanted you to take a more academic path, but that hardly means he deserved to be brutally killed?" Alice watched the woman closely.

"Is that what Ian said?" She rolled her eyes to the ceiling. "Where is he, anyway?"

"Your brother is living on an island in the Orkneys called North Dorga."

Her head whipped forward, genuine surprise showing on her face. "You're shitting me?"

"No, he's been there for a few years now, working on one of the farms. Why does that surprise you?"

Her expression closed down once again. "No reason. I just haven't been in contact for a while, that's all."

"Where were you on the 1st November, Billi?" Alice asked casually.

"Is that the day Dad was murdered? Well, the conference had just started, so I expect I was on one of the protests in the town centre. That's the reason I'm in Glasgow, to make sure these bloody politicians actually do something about climate change."

"Are there any witnesses that could back up your whereabouts?"

She snorted unpleasantly. "I was amongst hundreds of others. But would anyone remember me? Probably not."

"Are you involved with the Earth's Saviours movement? You were standing with them in George Square at the event a few days ago? Are you familiar with their wooden cross symbol? Your friend Harry helps to make them."

"*Harry* and his sister are members of ES," she almost spat out the name. "I've been to their offices a few times and help make banners. I'm sympathetic to their campaign but I'm not a member. I don't like to be part of a group. There are too many hangers-on who don't really understand what our true aims are."

"Did you know your father was a delegate at the climate conference? He worked for a children's charity that campaigned to protect young people around the world from the impact of climate change. Surely that was in sympathy with your aims, too?"

"No, I didn't know he was a delegate. My father had plenty of jobs that sounded worthy on paper. It didn't change who or what he was." Billi began examining her nails, the black varnish was chipping off.

"Did you know he worked in Africa for an education charity? He was there for six years?"

She shuffled in her seat. "Yeah, I did hear something. Mum told me, I think."

"Because you seem to know more about your father's career than you've been suggesting? What other jobs did he have that sounded, 'worthy on paper'?" Alice leant right forward, her gaze fixed on the woman opposite.

Sweat was beginning to bead at her brow. She shrugged out of her jacket, as if suddenly hot, revealing a t-shirt for an obscure band underneath. "No comment."

"Okay, so I'm assuming you'd followed your father's career quite closely. In that case, it seems hard for me to believe you didn't know he was in Glasgow this week. It would have been a good opportunity to catch up with your Dad, don't you think? He was in a position of authority and you want to promote your cause at COP26. If I were you, I'd be tempted to use my influence with him? Is that why you arranged to meet?"

Billi narrowed her eyes with undisguised hostility. "No comment."

Alice was about to say more about this, when her vision was drawn to Billi's exposed arm. Her skin was pale and freckly, but she could just discern a small tattoo on her wrist, in the place where you'd check for a pulse. "What's that?"

Billi automatically covered the area with her other hand. "It's a bloody tattoo. Never seen one before?"

"I'm just interested in the subject, that's all. Can I see it?"

"No, you bloody can't! What is this? Either arrest me for Dad's murder or let me go. You've got no evidence to keep me here – have you?"

Alice had to admit the woman was right. "We'll need you to provide us with the address of the friend you're staying with. Don't leave the country."

*

Alice and Andy watched as the woman pulled her jacket back on and left the police station.

"I've got a squad car outside that will keep tabs on her. Let's just hope the address she gave us was genuine. She was right, without any evidence to tie her to the murder we can't bring her in again. Thanks for helping me out, Andy."

Andy turned to face his colleague. "No problem. She's definitely got something to hide. What was all that about a tattoo?"

Alice shrugged her shoulders. "It was very small, but I could've sworn the tattoo on her wrist was in the shape of a tiny teddy bear."

Andy crinkled his brow in puzzlement.

“Come on, I’ll buy you a decent coffee and explain.”

Chapter 43

"I'm sorry I wasn't with you." Dermot was pacing the dusty ground outside their tent in Ntwara. "You shouldn't have been in that position, out there alone."

"The man wasn't of any danger to me. But if I hadn't been there, if Adam and I hadn't interrupted, Frank McCabe would have taken that boy away from his family by force."

Dermot ran a hand through his hair which was becoming highlighted by the sun. "I still don't get it. Why did this worker for 'Teaching Tanzania' think he could get away with that? It's certainly unethical and very probably illegal too."

"We didn't speak much in the jeep on the way back. To be honest, I was too shocked by what I'd seen. I also wanted Matthew to drive us back to camp before we challenged him on it. We were very vulnerable out there in the savannah. It wasn't the right place to be throwing around accusations."

"We still are," Dermot glanced about him at the tiny village, with the sun disappearing behind the rocky horizon. "We've got to be able to get back to Dodoma."

Sharon knew this was true, but she wasn't content to let the issue rest until they'd returned safely to the capital, she wanted answers now. "What did you find out when you questioned the other 'Teaching Tanzania' employees?"

"Most of them are just kids, straight out of university. They seemed genuinely devoted to the local children and their families. I can't see any of them employing the methods you witnessed."

"That Frank McCabe fella was well into his thirties, he's obviously been out here a good few years. Perhaps I witnessed a glimpse of the bad old days?"

"We need to speak with Matthew. Find out the truth." Dermot began walking in the direction of their guide's tent.

Sharon caught his arm. "We need to be careful. Remember that knife he's got in his belt?"

Dermot nodded, a grim expression on his face. He could picture it clearly.

*

Matthew was sitting in a fabric camp chair outside his tent, his long legs outstretched and a glass of amber liquid in his hand. "Dermot! Can I tempt you with another whisky? I've opened a new bottle?"

"No thanks." Dermot located another couple of chairs and the detectives sat down. "Sharon witnessed a very unpleasant incident this afternoon, when she visited the Hamisis' farm."

Matthew knocked back the contents of his glass, pouring some more from a bottle wedged in the sand by his feet. "Yes, Adam told me. I've had a word with Frank, reminded him of our guidelines. He won't be acting in that way again."

"But he's still working for you?" Sharon tipped her head quizzically.

"Frank has been with the charity for over ten years. He's a valued employee. Today he was stressed and exhausted from the heat. He deserves a second chance."

"When you have children coming to your school from farms several kilometres away, where do they stay? I'm assuming they aren't bused in and out each day?"

Matthew gripped his glass. "No, that wouldn't be practical. Those children from the wider countryside are put up by families in the village. We provide an allowance and food for them. They are very well cared for."

"So, how often do they see their own families?" Dermot asked.

"They go home at the end of each term. To be honest, the teachers often struggle when they return to class as they tend to work on the land during the holidays and forget much of what they have been taught. There aren't usually any books or writing materials at home."

"There must be a number of families who aren't happy for their children to be taken away to school like that? They're very young," Sharon persisted.

Matthew shook his head sadly. "Most families do what's best for their children in the end. We have an excellent interpreter who speaks with parents in Swahili. They all eventually agree. Many of these families live in terrible poverty, detective. We need to put the children first."

Sharon frowned. "Your charity has been operating for a long time. In the early days, were you so diligent about making sure there was parental permission for children to be taken away for schooling? What about Quentin Lester? What was his approach when he was out here?"

Matthew took a deep breath, as if controlling his emotions. "Quentin built the foundations for some of our schools with a pick axe and his bare hands. Thousands of children have been given improved life chances because of his hard work."

"That doesn't answer my question." Sharon continued to look at the man, whose eyes were unreadable in the encroaching dusk. The teeming wildlife had started up its low hum around them, as if passing judgement on the man's words themselves.

"Quentin was old fashioned in his approach.

When the families didn't agree for us to take the children, he used to get a local official to accompany him to the dwelling." He gulped another mouthful of whisky.

"And the children were taken away by force?" Dermot kept his tone even.

"There wasn't usually any force needed. With an official present, the family tended to hand the child over."

"But it wasn't what they wanted! They were just intimidated by these authority figures arriving on their doorstep!" Sharon felt bile rising in her throat.

Matthew tossed his empty glass onto the soft ground, getting to his feet. "You people swan in here with your western sensibilities, making judgements on the way we do things. If it were down to pen-pushers like you, with your endless rules and red tape, there'd be no schools out here in the countryside. Hundreds of children would have been denied an education!"

Dermot stood too, making sure the man didn't make a move for his belt. "Poor children from deprived communities deserve the same safeguards our own children do. Without that principle, no charity should function."

Matthew's posture sagged, as if the fight had gone out of him. "I *know* that. I'm disgusted by what Frank did today. It's not how Simon and Rehema run things now. That's why Quentin was sent home. One of the younger volunteers reported him to head office. They'd been uncomfortable with the way some of the children were being brought to the villages. So, Simon told him to leave." He raised his hands in frustration. "I didn't agree with his methods, but I can understand why he felt compelled to resort to them. Quentin believed with all his heart that he knew what was best for those children."

And there, Sharon thought sadly, was the reason Quentin Lester had been such a dangerous man.

"We will need to return to Dodoma as early as possible tomorrow," Dermot said firmly. "We've seen all we need to here."

"Of course," Matthew replied. "I'll wake you at first light."

Chapter 44

It was quiet on the floor of the serious crime division with so many of the team missing. Alice had called her remaining colleagues, plus DCI Bevan, to congregate around her desk, which without Sharon's ebullient presence, seemed oddly empty.

"I hope you don't mind me roping Andy in for the day, Ma'am?" Alice eyed her boss carefully, not wishing to disrupt the careful plans they'd made for this fortnight, before the murder of Quentin Lester had thrown them off track.

Andy added, "there aren't any demos planned for the next forty-eight hours. I've sent my officers home to get some kip before the action picks up again for the last few days of the conference."

"Not a problem," Dani said. "We need all hands on deck with this murder inquiry. My team has been scattered to the four winds as it is."

Andy smiled. "Sharon and Dermot are due to fly in late tonight. I got an email from Shaz this morning."

"So did I. They picked up some very interesting information out there. I'm glad they went." Dani beckoned the newest member of their team over to join them. "Andy, this is Klara Laska, she's a criminal analyst and has been looking into crimes similar to our murder."

Andy nodded a greeting, noting the woman's well-dressed poise. She was quite a different character to their usual go-to criminal psychologist, Rhodri Morgan; a scruffy university professor type who was now retired.

Alice cleared her throat. "After we released Billi Star yesterday afternoon, the surveillance team followed her to a property on Danes Drive,

Scotstoun. It seems the address she gave us was correct. The squad car is positioned outside, but she hasn't left the property yet."

"Just make sure there isn't a lane at the rear she can slip out through," Dani added. "My flat isn't far from there and plenty of the properties have ginnels running between them. We don't want her slipping away again."

"I'll radio the car and tell them to check round the back." Alice took a breath. "Elinor Lester changed her name by deed poll to 'Billi Star' five years ago. She doesn't have a criminal record under either name, nor does she have a driving licence or pay any taxes. There are no social media accounts which bear her name, although that doesn't mean she doesn't have one."

"She certainly lives 'off-grid'. It's unusual for a woman of her age," Dani commented. "You met her, did she strike you as someone who could have murdered her own father in the way he was found?"

"I know I'm new to this case, Ma'am," Andy replied, "but for what it's worth, I reckon she's hiding something. She's got no alibi for the day her dad was killed and she knew more about his recent activities than she was claiming. I think she's more than capable of murdering him. She really hated the guy."

Klara retrieved a photograph from the file she was holding. She showed it to Andy. "This is a still from the CCTV in the hotel corridor just before Lester was murdered. We think the figure behind him in that image is his killer. Could it be the woman you interviewed yesterday?"

Andy looked closely, he passed it to Alice. "She's tall and thin. It seems her hair changes colour more times than the traffic lights on the Clyde Gateway. But if she wore a thick dark coat, and had pulled the hood up to obscure her head, that could definitely be her."

Alice nodded. "I agree. It would also explain why Lester was so relaxed about taking this person up to his hotel room, if it was his own daughter."

Dani rested her weight on the edge of the desk. "Yes, but would she hate him enough to drive a stake through his heart, remove his clothes and place a gown on him after death? There must have been a moment when she had to watch him die. Could she really do that to her own father?"

It was Alice who replied. "I looked into her eyes in that interview yesterday. They are full of anger. I think she could've done it, yes. Then there was the tattoo on her wrist. I only got a fleeting glance, but I'm sure it was a tiny teddy-bear."

Klara produced another sheaf of papers. "Which brings us back to the murders in Wick and Inverness. I have been looking more closely into those."

Dani nodded in encouragement. "What did you discover?"

"Mabel Flett and Irene Vickers were pretty similar in age. Mabel Flett was working for Caithness and South Orkney council as an admin assistant when she was killed. Irene Vickers managed her own children's nursery on a new estate in Westhill. But Vickers hadn't always done that job. Twenty years ago, both women worked for the same council. In the child protection department."

Dani gave a start. "They were social workers?"

"Yes, at that time, they were based at the headquarters of the Caithness and South Orkney Council in Golspie, just off the A9."

"So they worked together? Does that mean they knew one another?" Alice felt her excitement building at this news.

Klara shrugged. "I couldn't get a confirmation, but it was a small department and the two women worked there for several years at the same time. They must have done."

"Yes, they must." Dani rubbed the back of her neck where tension was seizing up her muscles. "I'll have to inform the teams investigating both of their murders of this information. It potentially connects the two crimes and can't be ignored. There are barely any murders in the Highland region as it is and for two victims of violent crime to be known to one another means a coordinated investigation is required."

"Why didn't *they* find this connection?" Andy rolled his eyes, passing silent judgement on his provincial counterparts.

"Because nobody made the link until Dermot looked at the evidence. Neither team identified that the murder scenes had been staged. Irene Vickers' death had already been solved as far as Highlands and Islands were concerned. Staged murders are incredibly rare."

"You don't think the second woman's death was a traffic accident then?"

"Not now we are aware she and Mrs Flett knew one another and both had a teddy bear placed at the scene," Dani turned up her lip in disgust. "I believe someone followed Mrs Vickers that morning, waiting until the white van was stationary, or the lady was crossing the road. She was shoved to the ground and her coat wound around the bumper of the van. Then someone stuffed the teddy behind the fender before the vehicle drove away."

Alice shuddered. "Irene Vickers' body was then dragged along a tarmacked road for several kilometres. She had multiple head injuries. It was a horrific way to die."

“As was having your head held under bathwater until you drowned,” Klara added. “Or having a splintered piece of wood driven into your chest.”

Dani nodded. “Whoever killed these people was filled with hate. These murders were pre-planned and displayed absolutely no mercy for the victims.”

“So, what’s the link to Quentin Lester?” Andy asked. “That’s the case we need to focus on. One of these women was bound with a palm cross, which links to the cross that killed our man, I get that. But what is *his* link to these two women? Did the same person kill all three? Without knowing that, we’re no further forward.”

Dani didn’t have an answer to that. But once again, she knew Andy was absolutely right.

Chapter 45

The sun had tentatively broken through the dense cloud. Dan Clifton swung his legs out of the hotel bed and stretched his arms above his head. All he could hear on this bright morning were the cries of the sea birds soaring over the bay. The storm had finally broken.

The detectives packed their bags and left them by the reception desk. Hopeful they would receive news that the boat to Kirkwall was running.

Tyler kept his breakfast choice light, in anticipation of the journey. Although the wind had died down, he knew the sea that separated this small island from Mainland Orkney was treacherous for boats.

Dan sipped his coffee with a smile on his face. But he also felt unsettled, as if there were secrets on this island that they'd not managed to uncover. Their encounter with Hugh Turner had been deeply disturbing. Something had happened to the man to leave him so broken that Dan wanted desperately to understand. But it was neither their jurisdiction or their business to get involved.

Tyler dusted his hands clean of toast crumbs and got to his feet. As he did so, the landlord stepped into the lounge and announced, as if the place were full of clientele and didn't just contain the two policemen, "I've a telephone call for a DC Dan Clifton. You can take it out in the hall."

*

Tyler sat in the back seat of the Hilux with an expression of barely suppressed disappointment on his face. “What if the weather changes again and we’ve missed our chance to get off the island?”

Eddie called over his shoulder from the driver’s seat, where he was negotiating the peaks and troughs of the east road once again, “the weather is set fair for a few days at least. Not to worry on that score.”

Tyler set his mouth in a stubborn line, like a teenager enduring a trip they didn’t want to be on.

“The DCI has simply asked us to interview Ian once again, in light of the new evidence they’ve received about his father. It will only take a couple of hours.” A part of Dan was pleased they were staying, he felt there was unfinished business there.

As the truck pulled up to the courtyard of the farm, they could see that both the Land Rover and the delivery van were parked up by the barns. “Good,” Eddie exclaimed. “It looks like they’re all at home.”

Maggie Sinclair had seen them arrive and approached the three men from the door to her kitchen. “Morning, Eddie. What can I do for you today? We’ve finally got a day decent enough to let the animals back into the field. The boys have just come back down from there.”

“The Glasgow detective needs to speak with Ian again. It shouldn’t take long.”

A shadow passed across the woman’s face. “I don’t know what the lad could possibly still have to tell you, but you’ll find him in the kitchen with the others, having their cup of tea.”

Dan let Eddie lead the way. The kitchen table was filled with a large tea-pot and several mugs, plates filled with biscuits were scattered around them. Seated beside one another were Roy, Stevie and Ian. There was also a younger lad, who the detective assumed was Joe, standing by the stove, shovelling a slice of fruit cake into his mouth.

Dan decided to take charge, rather than let Eddie railroad his interview. “Ian, we’d like to have another word with you. In private.”

The young man placed his mug on the slab of worn oak. “Okay, but I’m not sure what else you want to know?”

“Why don’t you come outside in the sun? We can sit on the bench out there, get some fresh air?” Dan led Tyler out of the busy kitchen, not waiting for a reply. Thankfully, Ian soon followed.

Dan gestured for him to take a seat on the cast iron bench which faced out towards the still sea. “I’ve had fresh information from my DCI back in Glasgow. They’ve located your sister, who now calls herself, Billi Star.”

Ian twisted round on the bench. “Is she okay? Where is she living?”

“It seems that Billi is staying with a friend in the Glasgow area. She is in the city for the COP26 conference, to take part in the protests.”

He nodded to indicate that made sense. “Does she know about Dad? That he’s dead?”

“Yes, she was taken in to the station for an interview yesterday and was informed then. Your sister had no alibi for the day your father was murdered. She showed absolutely no remorse that he was dead.”

Ian ran a hand through his curly hair. “That’s just Elinor – or whatever she’s calling herself these days. My sister opted out of a conventional lifestyle years ago. She hated Dad, probably more than the rest of us.”

“Enough to have killed him? At the moment, your sister is our key suspect. She is the correct height and build for the person we have on CCTV accompanying your father to his hotel room minutes before he was murdered."

Ian's eyes widened. "I know she's gone off the rails, but my sister wouldn't *kill* anyone!?"

"But you've barely seen her in a decade," Tyler added. "What would you know about her now? It's really hard for us to understand why you are all so estranged. Nothing you've told us about your father really explains it?"

Ian rested his head in his hands and to the surprise of the detectives, he began to cry.

Chapter 46

When the young man's sobs had subsided, Dan placed a hand on his shoulder. "There's something you're not telling us, Ian. Your father has been brutally murdered and right now, your sister is our prime suspect. If there's stuff you've withheld from us, now is the time to share it."

"But Maggie and Roy don't know. If I tell you everything, I could lose my job here." He lifted his tear stained face. "They aren't just my employers, you know? They are my family."

Dan made his tone as sympathetic as possible. "The Sinclairs seem to really care for you. I'm sure that whatever you say, they'll understand and forgive."

Ian shook his head vigorously. "I'm not so sure. This entire island was traumatised twenty years ago by what happened. If they find out I'm connected to it, I'll have to leave and never come back." The sobs wrenched his body once more.

"We need to know what you're referring to, Ian. Two women of a similar age to your dad were killed in the Highlands in the last few years. We think their deaths are linked to your dad's murder. Both women had worked as social workers for Caithness and South Orkney Council twenty years ago. North Dorga was part of their jurisdiction. Does this have something to do with the events you're talking about?" Dan asked gently.

"Christ! Do you mean those two social workers were murdered! Just like Dad!" He glanced frantically about him, as if the answers would be provided by the landscape itself.

"Yes, we are coming to think so. But we don't know what connected these three people, only that there were methods in the way they were killed that linked the deaths. But I think you and your sister might know. Is that right?"

Ian seemed to have pulled himself together. A stillness had replaced the raw emotion. "Yes, we do know. Or can certainly offer a suggestion. If I tell you, my life here will be over, but if I don't, there will be a killer out there who won't ever be brought to justice."

"I think you know what you need to do, Ian."

He nodded, his body sagging with despondency. "Yes, I believe I do."

*

Sharon's face was still pink with sunburn. Whereas Dermot's skin had turned a pleasant olive tone and his hair had tinted blond in the powerful African sun.

"It looks like you pair are back from a week in the Maldives!" Andy commented jovially, as the two detectives walked towards their desks at Pitt Street.

Sharon laughed. "We wish, Andy!" She gave her colleague a cheerful wink, but didn't feel as jolly as she was making out. The trip to Africa had made a profound impression upon her.

Dermot laid his jacket on the back of his chair. "I tell you what, it's bloody freezing here in Glasgow."

"Aye," Andy called over, "it's all very well grabbing some winter sun, away from the Scottish winter. Only problem is, you've got to come back."

This comment was greeted with a few titters from other desks.

"But seriously," Andy continued. "I hear you two found out some important stuff over there. Good job."

Dermot nodded. "Is the DCI in her office, we need

to have a de-brief?"

Andy didn't get a chance to respond. Dani swung open the door to her office, letting it hit the wobbly partition with a bang. She marched out into the middle of the office floor.

"Great! DI Muir, DS Moffett, you're back. We need to get the entire team together for a briefing. I've just had a call from Dan Clifton on North Dorga. With the information he's just given me, it's going to be all hands on deck."

Chapter 47

Dani stood in front of their digital smartboard. "I'm not sure if you recall the press coverage at the time, but in 2001, there was a supposed, 'child abuse scandal' out on the Orkneys. Several families were involved." A newspaper front page filled the screen. The headline read; 'children removed from homes after suspicion of ritual abuse'.

Andy creased his brow in concentration. "I think I remember it. Weren't there a lot of kiddies taken into care? I recall my old ma' saying it was a 'witch-hunt' against the poor parents."

Dani nodded. "That was the case, yes. And your mother was absolutely right. The voice of common sense. Unfortunately, common sense had completely deserted Caithness and South Orkney social services during that period."

A memory forced itself to the front of Sharon's brain. "Wasn't there talk in the media of satanic abuse and paedophile rings?"

"Yes. I'll supply you all with the police and court reports relating to the incident in due course, but in the meantime, I'll provide a précis." She took a deep breath. "It began in March 2001, when a schoolgirl at the primary school on North Dorga told her teacher she was a victim of abuse. This girl was eight years old and a member of the Laughton family. They lived on a farm to the west of the island and there were three brothers and two sisters."

"The girl's testimony was recorded by a social worker who came over from Golspie on the mainland to conduct the interview. There were no other trained professionals on the island to deal with such an allegation. Her name was Irene Vickers. The authorities had already been concerned about this particular family, as the children were visibly malnourished and often missed school."

"So, Irene Vickers was involved in the Orkney child abuse case?" Klara was taking notes as the DCI spoke.

"Yes, and she wasn't the only one. Scotland has a unique child protection system, instated under a law of 1968. When an allegation of abuse is made, the local authority will set up so-called, 'children's panels' where the child's evidence will be considered by an independent, 'lay-person'. This panel may then apply to the sheriff for a 'place of safety' order to allow social services to remove a child. Needing an extra pair of hands, Irene was joined on the case by her colleague from Golspie, Mabel Flett."

"What happened in the case of the Laughton child?" Alice asked.

"The Laughton girl gave evidence to such a panel, she claimed sexual abuse by her father and her brothers. All the children were interviewed and later removed to the care of social services." Dani sighed. "But it didn't end there. A couple of particularly zealous social workers, believed to be Vickers and Flett, continued to interview the children even after their removal. A later Crown investigation described these interviews as 'relentless' and 'manipulative'. A man who worked for the department lodged a complaint against his colleagues, his identity was protected in the report. He claimed the social workers were guilty of 'repeated coaching' when they interviewed the children. Basically, they were telling the kids what to say and putting ideas in their heads."

"Which is bloody abuse in itself," Andy grunted.

"During one of these sessions, one of the Laughton children suggested they'd been abused by other men on North Dorga; that his father had been part of some kind of paedophile ring."

"This wasn't true?" Klara asked.

"The later Crown Investigation concluded these claims were entirely unjustified and very likely suggested by the social workers themselves in their zeal to root out child abuse."

"So, what happened before someone finally intervened?" Alice asked sadly.

Dani's face was set in a grim mask. "Seven families on the island were identified as being part of this child abuse ring, based on the evidence of the Laughton child. The social workers set out to gather evidence against the parents; through interviews with the children and neighbours and searches of their homes. The majority of these families were English settlers to the island, without well-established roots or a support network to speak up for them."

"Was the investigation based on prejudice, do you think?" Dermot asked. "Against the English?"

Dani shrugged. "I think there must have been an element of it, even if it was just subconscious on the part of the accusers. But the impact was devastating. The sheriff granted 'place of safety' orders for each of the children in these families. They were taken from their homes by social workers during a dawn raid on 20th February 2002."

Sharon shook her head in disbelief, imagining the scene she'd witnessed at the farm in the Masasi savannah, with little Mohammed being wrenched from his mother's arms. The parallel was painful to acknowledge. "How could that be allowed to happen? With so little evidence?"

"I think there was a sense at the time, that the testimony of the children was entirely genuine and uncoached. It wasn't until one of the social workers blew the whistle and the families on Dorga launched a national campaign to have their children returned, that doubts were raised about the methods used." Dani took a step forward and made eye contact with every member of her team. "There was another reason the accusations gained credence too. An elected councillor from Inverness, who also worked for a youth housing and education charity that had run summer schools on North Dorga for the local children in previous years, read about the child abuse cases in the local paper and decided to offer his services as the 'lay official' who would preside over the child panels and review the evidence. It was felt he was a trustworthy local figure who would give the Sheriff his impartial assessment. His name was Quentin Lester."

Chapter 48

Eddie had agreed to give them a lift further along the east road to the lighthouse. The sun was glistening above the tower, making the blue and white structure appear almost pretty, certainly in contrast to how forbidding the headland had looked during their previous visit.

Dan and Tyler climbed out of the Hilux, leaving Ian hunched over in the backseat for the time-being, with Eddie keeping an eye on the lad. Dan took a deep breath and approached the final cottage in the row.

The detective didn't need to knock. Hugh Turner emerged along the side passage of the cottage, a spade in his hand. "I thought I told you two to sling your hooks! What the hell are you doing back here!"

Dan almost expected the man to wave his spade at them, but thankfully he didn't. "We are very sorry to disturb you again, Mr Turner. But we know more about your story now. I'm so very sorry about the ordeal you went through twenty years ago. We are here to talk with you about it. Even after all this time has passed, we might be able to help." Dan braced himself for another barrage of abuse. Instead, he was surprised to see Hugh's eyes grow damp.

"I don't know what the hell you think you can do now," he said gruffly. "My Rachel's dead and my children are long gone." His posture slumped, the fight seeming to have gone out of him.

"Can we come in and talk?" Dan took a tentative step along the path.

Hugh shrugged. "Why the hell not? You're the first folk to have shown any interest in over a decade."

Dan allowed the man to lead them around the

back of the property and in through the kitchen door. They took seats around a small pine table. Tyler was relieved to note Hugh had left the door ajar, which was helping to dissipate the cloying smell of decay.

"Do you want a cup of tea?"

Dan shook his head. "No, Mr Turner. We just want to hear your story."

The older man sunk down lower into his seat, as if wishing it would swallow him up. "You obviously know some of it already. Rachel and I had moved to North Dorga from Yorkshire twenty-two years ago. I was a teacher and Rachel had been a freelance journalist. We thought by moving out here and being able to buy without a mortgage, we could give up our work eventually and become self-sufficient. I was going to do up this house and Rach could write a series of articles about us starting a new life out here. She'd already been given a commission by a lifestyle magazine."

Dan nodded his encouragement. "Lots of families do the same."

"Kirsty and Sam had settled in really well at the primary school. Our first couple of winters had been tough, but we were getting used to it, starting to make some good friends. A lady in one of the other cottages, Nicola, even took the children to school with her kids every day. She worked in St Martin."

Dan said nothing, allowing the man to continue. He noticed the crack in his voice when he mentioned the kids and hoped he'd be able to continue.

"We had no idea what was coming, no warning. We'd heard about the children who'd been taken into care over on the west side of the island, but it had nothing to do with us, or so we thought. Apparently, one of the Laughton kids had mentioned my name to a social worker, a couple of months after she'd been removed from the family home. She'd suggested I'd been at her house, socialising with her father. A frequent visitor, even." He gripped the arms of his chair until the knuckles of his hands went white. "I'd never even met the man. It was total bullshit."

"The inquiry concluded it was the social workers themselves who suggested your name and those of other men on the island to the children. The accusations against you were entirely baseless."

Hugh's eyes flashed. "I know that! But it didn't stop those women coming and taking my children away, whilst my wife was still in her bed! Kirsty tried to resist, she held onto the sink in the bathroom upstairs. The woman pulled her so hard the damn thing came loose, spraying cold water all over the place."

Dan shook his head in disgust.

"Of course, Sam was too small to fight back. The other woman dragged him out of Rach's arms – his own mother!"

To his surprise, Tyler felt tears forming in his own eyes. These children were his contemporaries. He could barely imagine what it would've been like to have been taken from his own parents at that age. He was still really close to his mum.

Hugh fixed both officers with a steely stare. "And two policemen stood and watched it happen, along with that councillor. They just stood by and allowed our children to be wrenched violently from their own home. They even held me and my wife back whilst the others drove away. What I couldn't believe and would make me laugh if the whole affair hadn't ruined all our lives, was that they brought a little teddy bear with them. It was wearing a red bow. As if a *soft-toy* would make our children happy to be taken from their mum and dad!"

"I'm sorry. The social workers had an order from

the sheriff, that's all I can say in the defence of those officers who were present. They had a court order preventing them from intervening."

"Oh yes, the *'place of safety order'*. I've still got it to this day, sitting in a drawer. I thought at the time that I'd get a lawyer to fight it, to pick it apart word by word. But it turned out the law didn't apply in our situation. The social services department operated in their own kind of 'wild west', where evidence and reason had been abandoned."

Dan could feel this man's anger radiating around the room like an alternative form of energy. It hadn't lessened in all these years. He lowered his tone, knowing his next question was a difficult one. "Many of the other families accused of abuse had their children returned to them within six months. Why didn't that happen for you and Mrs Turner?"

Hugh rubbed his face with a grubby, calloused hand. "We got ourselves a lawyer straight away, of course. Much of the so-called 'evidence' they'd found in the houses they searched were ludicrous – my old academic gown was considered a black cloak used in 'satanic rituals', a bunch of Easter crosses in another families' place was also seen as a satanic symbol. They even took away the kiddies' toy swords and daggers. Someone in authority had completely lost their marbles. Those charges were easy to refute, but it still took months for most of the kids to get returned. When they did, the families quickly moved away, probably regretting the day they'd set foot on this desolate mound of soil."

Dan exchanged a glance with Tyler at the mention of the gown and the crosses. "But you're still here."

"Yes, I am. Someone in the council at the time decided to investigate my career as a teacher, back in Sheffield. What they discovered, was that a pupil had once made an accusation against me. Said I'd kept them behind after class, propositioned them. The case had been thoroughly investigated at the time and no charges brought. In fact, the pupil dropped the accusation in the end. She'd been going through a difficult time at home, developed a crush on me. It happens."

"So, how could the authorities use this against you? If the charges had been dropped?"

"You don't seem to know how child services operates, detective. All they need is a 'suspicion' that a child is in danger to allow them to be removed. There is a far lower threshold for evidence than there would be in a criminal case."

Dan gasped. "And this meant you never had your children returned to you? Because of an unproven charge in the past?"

Hugh blew air out of his cheeks. "Seems unbelievable, doesn't it? But taken together with the accusation made by the Laughton child, it appeared irrefutable to the authorities. Lightning doesn't strike twice, does it? I'm pretty sure there are people still on this island who believe I abused my own children and that's why they were never returned to me and Rachel." A sob finally escaped and the tears began to fall.

Dan was concerned his own voice would reveal the emotion he felt at hearing this man's tragic story. "Why did you stay, Hugh? Nobody would have blamed you if you'd left this place and never returned."

He wiped the snot and tears from his face, not caring about social niceties. "Because Rachel wanted to stay. She couldn't leave without the children. She died of cancer a couple of years ago. The grief ate her up inside. I'd kept the place up until my wife was gone. But now I don't bother. Who would it be for?"

"For *yourself*, Mr Turner. You deserve a life too."

The man shook his head, as if the idea was inconceivable.

Dan took a deep breath. "We've something else to tell you. Young Ian Lester is waiting in the car. I know he's been helping out with the house over the last couple of years. The thing is, the local councillor who assisted in building a case against you and your wife; who stood in this house whilst your children were taken, Quentin Lester, he was Ian's father. When Ian found out about his father's role in it all, many years ago, he was disgusted, as were his wife and daughter. They barely spoke to him again. I think Ian came back here to make amends in some way, for the mistakes of his dad."

Hugh glanced up. "Oh, we know about that. Maggie, Roy and I worked out who the boy was as soon as he said his name. We didn't know if he had any idea about what his dad had done, but it didn't matter. The boy wanted to do some good. We weren't about to judge him for that."

Dan was surprised, but then he'd sensed Maggie knew something, had been trying to protect the boy from their questions. "He's outside in the truck with Eddie. He wanted to explain why he came here, ask for your forgiveness."

"Jeez, there's nothing to forgive. Ian didn't choose his father. I suppose that I should be glad Lester lost his children too, like it was some kind of natural justice. But it doesn't help, not one bit."

Dan said no more, but led Hugh out of the house and down the front path to where the Hilux was parked. Eddie and Ian were now standing on the gritted road, facing towards the dilapidated cottage with pensive expressions on their faces.

Hugh strode purposefully towards the young man, taking him into his arms without hesitation. "I don't bloody care who your father was, you daft sod," he muttered into his shoulder. Ian collapsed into Hugh's embrace, the relief seeming to take all of the strength out of him.

Dan watched the scene from the path, not caring that tears were streaking down his own cheeks, flowing entirely unchecked.

Chapter 49

The clock on the wall of the serious crime floor was showing 4.30pm. Alice glanced up at it and cursed under her breath. She'd been working flat out to research every family that had been affected by the North Dorga child abuse scandal in 2002, trying to discover where they were now. The entire team had. The task had been so absorbing, the time had run away with her.

The undertaking was incredibly difficult, as some of the children had been given new names if they'd been adopted by a different family. She couldn't think about that now, she needed to pick Charlie up from nursery. Fergus was in Edinburgh overnight for a case so there was no one else who could go.

The DI grabbed her coat and muttered a hurried goodbye to her colleagues, themselves still hunched over a laptop screen, feverishly taking notes.

The traffic had slowed to a crawl on London Road. Alice struck the wheel in frustration. Finally, she reached the lights and just about managed to accelerate through the intersection before they turned red. When she reached the street where Cragganhall Community Centre nursery was situated, she found a space by the pavement with ease, which meant she was late.

Alice slammed the car door and jogged through the wrought iron gates to the reception area. She spoke to the woman seated behind the Perspex screen. "I'm so sorry I'm late. I got held up at work. I'm here to pick up Charlie Kelso."

The woman narrowed her eyes, confusion flashing briefly across her face. "Let me just go and check," she said warily.

Alice waited in the corridor for several minutes. A

sense of unease building in her chest. What the hell was taking so long?

One of the nursery teachers emerged from a side office. “Mrs Kelso?”

“It’s DI Mann actually. What’s the problem?“

The woman looked uncomfortable. “I’m afraid Charlie isn’t here. He was picked up twenty minutes ago by a lady. Carmel tells me that you called this afternoon to confirm that she would be fetching him as you were held up at work?”

Alice felt the blood pumping so hard in her ears she could barely hear what the woman was saying. “What? I did no such thing!? You let a stranger take my son? He’s just a baby!”

The teacher raised her hands as if she were defending physical blows. “There’s been a terrible misunderstanding. I think we’d better call the police. I’ll go and get the manager.”

Alice felt her legs might buckle beneath her. She put a hand out to rest against the wall, her heart drumming in her chest. “I *am* the bloody police,” she just about managed to rasp.

*

Dani and Andy arrived at the nursery school within twenty minutes. Dermot and Sharon had abandoned their research into the 2002 victims of the abuse scandal and were instead initiating an amber alert for a missing child, making sure every squad car in the city was out searching for him.

Alice was slumped in a plastic chair opposite the reception desk when the detectives arrived. Dani held up her warrant card and demanded to see the receptionist.

The middle-aged woman, her face pinched with anguish, was called Carmel Minton. “I’m so sorry. I just can't believe this has happened. We ask parents to call in during the day if there is going to be someone new picking up their child. That's exactly what happened in this case. I genuinely thought it was Charlie's mum who was speaking."

"But you've got no real idea who is calling, do you? It's not a very fail safe system, is it?" Dani could feel her frustration building, but there was no point in berating this woman. It wouldn't help find Charlie. The manager emerged from a back office. She was in her forties and wore a smart suit. "I'm Laura Pike. You must be DCI Bevan?" She shook her head mournfully. "This is a really awful situation. I can only deeply apologise -"

Dani cut her off. "You'll have to do more than that. I assume there are CCTV cameras at the entrance to the school?"

"Yes and out in the playground."

"My colleague over there will need to view the recordings from 4.45pm today. Can you organise that now?"

She nodded, seeming to realise her soft soap words would be futile.

"I also need to take a statement from Mrs Minton. I assume it was you who handed the child over to this woman?"

The receptionist nodded, tears now beginning to pool in her eyes as she grasped the enormity of her mistake.

Dani turned back to the corridor. Andy was seated beside Alice, his hand resting on her shoulder. The DI seemed to be in shock.

Dani crouched down on her haunches in front of her friend. "Alice, I'm going to need you to call Fergus and tell him what has happened. Is there any way he might have sent someone to pick Charlie up? Perhaps he was worried you'd be too busy?"

Alice shook her head. "No, he's in court today and tomorrow. On those occasions it's understood that I will do all the drop-offs and pick-ups. I should have been here in time, if only I'd left the station ten minutes earlier." She looked Dani in the eye, her gaze almost manic. "How could I have been so selfish? So neglectful?"

Dani placed her hand on Alice's knee. "Come on. That's crazy. Every parent gets held up at work from time to time. Now, I need you to stay focused for me, stop blaming yourself and start blaming the person who took him. Try to think of anything unusual that has happened recently. Has anyone approached you and Charlie that seemed suspicious? Anyone showing a particular interest in him?"

Alice leapt to her feet, almost sending the DCI toppling backwards. "Of course! That woman! She was leaning over Charlie in the back of my car, the day it was raining. Then I saw her in the lift at the offices of Earth's Saviours. I'm sure she's been watching us! Now she's taken my son!"

Chapter 50

Sharon shoved aside the pile of papers on her untidy desk. Her heart was breaking for what Alice was going through but she needed to keep her mind on the job. Dermot came to stand beside her. "The boss has just sent through the statement from the school receptionist. We've got a description from her which matches with the one Alice gave of this woman who approached her and Charlie last week."

Sharon opened her inbox and scanned the details. "It sounds just like the woman we saw in the lift of the building on Castle Street. I saw her too. She was about 5'5", had shoulder-length brown hair she wore in a twisted bun. She was dressed in a black coat and wore a skirt, tan tights and low heels. Much like the descriptions given here. I'm sure it's her."

"Then she must work in that building. We need a list of all their personnel right now."

Sharon nodded. "Alice and I wanted to try and find out who she was but we didn't feel we had enough evidence to approach an employer. She hadn't actually done anything at that time, just acted suspiciously."

"Well, she's done something now," Dermot added solemnly.

*

Dani and Andy were bent over a small screen that was replaying the CCTV footage. The playground was busy. Parents and younger siblings were milling about everywhere before the bell sounded for the end of the school day.

"It looks like chaos," Dani muttered.

"Carol works in a similar nursery, on the other

side of town. It's always like that at pick-up. I'm amazed anyone goes home with their own kid."

Dani stared at the rolling footage. "There!" She cried. "Freeze the frame."

Andy paused the film. He could see a woman in smart office clothes approaching the entrance doors. She looked quite different from the other mums in their casual-wear and designer yoga pants.

"Let's see what she does now."

Andy allowed the film to run. The woman disappeared into the building, emerging a few minutes later holding the hand of a tiny, dark-haired child, a rucksack on his back. "Shit, there they are."

All the detectives could do was watch helplessly as the black figure led Alice's son out of the gates and away from the range of the camera.

"Can we see which direction she goes in?"

"I'm not sure. But she's walking at quite a pace. Do you think she put him in a vehicle?"

"Alice said she's only seen this woman on foot. We have to hope to God they are only walking distance away, otherwise they could be bloody anywhere."

Andy thought about his own daughter, older than Charlie but still just primary age, she'd be at home now with Carol, having her tea. His stomach dropped like a stone.

*

The solicitor's firm that had offices on the third floor of the building where Earth's Saviours had their headquarters were proving very helpful. Sharon had been emailed a list of their current personnel and a friendly HR manager informed her that one member of their staff was at that time on a week's annual leave. Her name was Kirsty Turner.

Sharon put down the phone and called Dermot over from his desk. "I may have a name! The HR lady is just sending me her address and phone number. It's amazing how quickly people respond when a child is missing, although the manager did say she couldn't possibly imagine this employee would be involved."

Dermot creased his brow. "What was that name again?"

"Kirsty Turner. She's 32 years old."

Dermot jogged back to his desk and grabbed a sheet of notes. "I thought so," he called back. "Kirsty Turner is the name of Hugh Turner's daughter; the man who Dan and Tyler interviewed on North Dorga. Kirsty was removed from her family in February 2002 at the age of twelve. It can't be a coincidence, can it?"

Sharon rose to her feet. "No, it bloody can't be. We need to get that address and fast."

Chapter 51

Sleet had begun to fall as the squad car pulled up outside the ground floor flat on Dalton Street. Dani had posted a couple of officers in the next-door neighbour's garden. The owner was happy to oblige when they heard a child was missing and perhaps being held in the adjacent property.

Alice had insisted she come along. Although Dani thought it was a bad idea, she'd allowed the DI to sit in the backseat, where she had promised to remain.

Andy climbed out of the passenger seat into the bitter cold. Dani joined him as he pulled open the gate and walked up to the front door. "We're only a couple of streets from Alice and Fergus's place," she commented under her breath.

Andy pressed the bell. They had back-up officers lingering further along the street, but didn't want to go in heavy handed if there was any risk the woman might hurt the child. There were protocols for this kind of thing.

When there was no answer, Andy hammered on the wooden panel. He turned to Dani and shook his head. The DCI spoke into her radio and within seconds, a line of officers streamed down the path, one of them wielding a metal ramrod, which he swung decisively at the old door, knocking it straight off its hinges.

The officers swarmed inside. The flat was neat and tidy. Dani entered the living room and looked around. There was no sign a young child had been in there. The sofa was accessorised with patterned cushions, all propped up immaculately along the backrest. A couple of paperbacks were piled evenly on a coffee table.

One of the officers tromped down the narrow

staircase. “No sign of them upstairs, Ma’am.”

Dani muttered an expletive under her breath. If they weren’t at the woman’s flat, where the hell where they? She strode out of the front door and marched down the path, stopping dead in her tracks when she saw Alice standing by the gate, her mobile phone in her hand, her face a deathly shade of pale.

“I’ve had a call,” she said shakily. “I think I know where they are.”

*

Andy was behind the wheel of the squad car. Whenever the traffic thickened, he turned on the ‘blue and twos’ to rush them through.

“I’ve called for an ambulance to meet us there,” Dani called into the back of the car. “What time did Macy McAdams call you?”

Alice was shaking uncontrollably. “About eight minutes ago.”

“Okay, we’ll be there in five. Now, Macy said she saw a figure out on the rooftop of the building. What’s the layout up there?”

Alice was trying hard to prevent her brain from recreating every possible sickening scenario in glorious technicolour. She had to remain calm, for the sake of her son. “There’s a huge loft space which spans the entire building. From what I remember, there are a couple of skylights in the roof itself, up in the rafters. That must be how she climbed out there, although I’ve no idea how she managed to do it unseen.” The words stuck in her craw.

“Right. I’ve instructed Macy to empty the loft space of people. Then we can get a better look ourselves. There may be another way to gain access to the roof. If Kirsty works there, she will probably know it.”

Alice shuddered. “The building is four storeys high.” The words came out as a whisper.

"We'll be there in minutes. I'm going to do everything I can. Okay?"

Alice nodded.

Dani's phone began to buzz. She lifted it to her ear. "Hi, Sharon. Good, now listen. I need every single piece of information you have on this woman." The DI listened in silence for a few moments before ending the call.

Andy screeched the car to all halt at the kerbside. "We're here."

Dani reached into the backseat and squeezed Alice's hand. "I need you to remain in the car. Under no circumstances are you to come out, whatever happens. Is that understood?"

The DCI leapt from the vehicle before her friend had time to answer.

Chapter 52

Macy McAdams had done as instructed and the loft space at the top of the building was completely deserted. The polished wood floors were strewn with half completed banners and the organisation's trademark makeshift wooden crosses lay in piles everywhere. Dani knew all the environmentalist groups were planning another series of marches and demonstrations in the final few days of the conference.

There were four officers with the DCI, including Andy. She turned to her old friend. "I'm going to climb out of that central skylight. I want you to follow behind, but keep a safe distance.

"Understood," he replied.

One of the other officers said, "we could see her out on the roof, Ma'am. It looks like she's holding the little boy. A parapet runs around the roofline. There's a fire escape that runs up the rear of the building, but it looks unsafe, a few of the lower bolts are missing. I reckon she climbed up that way with the boy, to avoid being seen. But you're better off using the skylight."

"Thanks, I don't think we've got time for anything else to be honest. Are the medics on standby?"

"Yes, Ma'am."

Dani took a deep breath, stood on one of the plastic chairs and hauled herself up through the open hatch.

The wind caught her full in the face. The sleet had stopped but the air was damp and cold. Dani edged her way around the parapet, keeping her body close to the angle of the tiled roof. Only a low iron rail stood between her and the drop below. As she turned a corner, so she was now facing the front of the building, she could see a figure up ahead with what looked like a bundle held in her arms. The pair looked dangerously close to the edge.

Dani shuffled along a little faster. When she felt she was in hearing range, she stopped, holding her hands up to show she was unarmed. "Kirsty! Can you hear me?"

The figure whipped round. "What are you doing here!?" She demanded.

"My name is Detective Chief Inspector Danielle Bevan. I'm here because we're worried about Charlie. His mum is downstairs, she wants to take him home. He needs to have his tea soon."

The woman's face creased in concentration. "You're the policewoman who was on the news, the one who created those safe walking routes through the city?"

"Yes, that's me. I hope it was helpful to you. I just want to help you now, if I can."

"My grandfather was one of the 'Bevin Boys', I know it's not the same spelling, but I felt connected to you."

Dani edged closer. "The miners who provided coal during the war? Yes, my dad told me all about them. He was a teacher, retired now."

"My dad is too, or he used to be. Although, I've not seen him for years and years. I was in care, you see. My parents were a danger to me and my brother. It was safer for us to be way from them, even though I didn't like the children's homes." She gripped the boy more tightly, who looked to be fast asleep in her arms.

"Is Charlie okay?" Dani was concerned about how floppy he looked.

"Yes, he's fine. I can look after him. I'm very organised. I'd never be late to pick him up, not like the policewoman with the red hair. She left him in the car you know. Anyone could have taken him."

Dani didn't wish to point out the irony of this statement. "You've only seen Alice when she's rushing at the end of the day. The rest of the time she's a brilliant mum. Charlie's dad loves him too. They are a family. It's important for them to be together."

Kirsty Turner flinched at these words. "I thought my family was safe. I believed they loved me and my brother, but the social workers told us they weren't good people, they wanted to hurt us. Appearances can be deceptive."

Dani shook her head. "Your parents *did* love you. The social workers made an awful mistake. You should have been returned to your mum and dad. Did nobody ever tell you that?"

Kirsty began jerking her body fiercely. "My social worker said mistakes were made with other families, but my dad was a bad man and we couldn't ever go back." Tears were escaping onto her wind-chapped cheeks. "But I hadn't remembered him that way. No matter how hard I tried, I couldn't recall him ever doing bad things to us."

Dani inched closer. "That's because he never did. Your dad was falsely accused. He'd had a complaint made against him when he was a teacher, before you went to North Dorga, but it was never proved. The social workers used this as a reason to take you away. It should never have happened. If you come back with me to the station I can explain properly."

Kirsty shook her head violently. "I don't understand!" The bundle in her arms was swinging dangerously close the edge.

Dani reached out. "I don't think you want to hurt Charlie, you're just confused about what happened to you. If you give the boy to me, we can work this out. None of it is your fault."

Kirsty looked at the DCI properly for the first time, her face streaked with tears and twisted with anguish.

Dani took one more step and placed her arms around the boy firmly. Kirsty leant back in surprise, but released her grip on the child and allowed the detective to take him. Dani spun around and handed the boy straight to Andy, who was hovering close behind. She turned back to the woman, who had now slumped down against the arch of the roof, her face a blank mask, shivering in the biting chill.

Dani leant down and enveloped Kirsty Turner in an embrace. "We'll take you back to the police station now. We will get you a counsellor and recommend a decent lawyer. It's time you got some proper answers after all these years."

Chapter 53

The flat felt warm as Dani entered. She kicked off her shoes and hung her jacket on a hook in the hall. Her limbs were so heavy she could barely make it to the kitchen, stopping instead in the front sitting room and collapsing onto the sofa.

James's athletic frame filled the doorway. "How are you?" There was genuine concern in his voice.

"Exhausted but immensely relieved."

"Can I get you a drink?"

"Yep, anything that's been distilled for more than five years please."

James smiled, moving to a mahogany drinks cabinet and pouring them both a generous measure of ten year old single malt.

Dani knocked back a mouthful. "Thanks, I bloody needed that."

James sat beside her, cradling the heavy glass in his hands. "How's the boy?"

"He's staying overnight in the paediatric wing of the Royal Infirmary. Kirsty Turner gave him a fentanyl tablet dissolved in a beaker of squash. She'd been prescribed the drug after a minor operation last year. The doctors say he'll be fine but will need to sleep it off. Otherwise he's unharmed, just a little chilled from his rooftop adventure."

James sighed. "Poor Alice and Fergus, they must have been beside themselves."

"Yes, Fergus has been granted an adjournment on his trial. He'll be back at home for the next few days at least. I've told Alice to take a week's compassionate leave."

"It's difficult to fathom how long it would take to get over a trauma like that." James sipped his whisky.

“Charlie will be fine. He slept through much of it. He won’t even remember what happened. It will haunt his parents for a good while though.”

“What will the woman be charged with?”

“Child abduction and assault, for the drug she gave him. She’s in one of the cells at Pitt Street right now. But a counsellor is going to give her an assessment first thing and her employers are sending out one of their solicitors to advise her. Apparently, the abduction is totally out of character. She’s been an exemplary employee there for years.”

“I’m not an expert in criminal law, but I reckon she’ll be assessed as a psychiatric admission. It’s absolutely awful what happened to her family. I’m sure if I told Sally the details, she’d be keen to represent them in a claim for damages. She’s into good causes these days. I’m amazed they hadn’t done so sooner.”

Dani sighed. “Kirsty was only twelve years old when she was removed from the family. She endured hours of questioning by social workers intent on planting the idea into her head she’d been abused. Despite being so young, she was still considered old for adoption. Kirsty went to a few foster families but ended up spending most of her childhood in residential homes.”

“What about her brother, were they kept together?”

Dani gave a humourless grunt. “Because the evidence from the Laughton case suggested abuse between siblings, the local authority decided all the children removed from homes in North Dorga should be kept apart. Sam Turner was only eight and a family adopted him within a few months, but his name was changed to that of his new family. Sharon is finding it difficult to track him down as a result.”

James polished off his dram. “It’s inhuman, to

separate a family like that on such scant evidence."

"Yes, it is. But a kind of madness had swept through the social services department that dealt with the case. Also, I think they fell under the influence of Councillor Quentin Lester. From what Sharon and Dermot told me about what he was up to in Tanzania, he had a long history of removing children from their parents."

"But *why*?"

Dani walked to the cabinet and re-filled their glasses. "He clearly had some kind of superiority complex. Lester seemed to genuinely believe he knew what was best for these children and that their families were somehow ignorant and lacking. He probably felt that in some cases, the State was better positioned to raise children than their own parents; if they seemed to him to be foolish or unworthy. I expect it masked deep insecurities of his own. As it was, his own children deserted him. But his working life was like a crusade, one that set out to 'save' children from their circumstances."

"It was a horribly misguided crusade. Why the hell wasn't he discredited after the whole Orkney debacle?"

"The crown investigation highlighted faults in a number of processes and systems within the local authorities involved, but placed no blame on any individuals. Like you say, it would probably have been up to families like the Turners to launch legal proceedings against the department, which would have placed blame with the individuals responsible. In the case of 'Teaching Tanzania', when his boss realised the methods Lester was using, he ended his contract, sending him off to another charity job with a glowing reference. If nobody is prepared to blow the whistle, these people never get unmasked for what they really are."

"It isn't so easy in reality to raise a civil case, especially when social services can point to the 'so-called' evidence they'd gathered against the family. And whistle-blowers tend to find their future job prospects seriously curtailed." James leant his body against Dani's. "If I'm honest, I can sort of see why someone wanted him dead, and those two social workers."

Dani hated to admit out loud that she could too. "Well, we started out with no motive for the bizarre murder of Quentin Lester, now we have a list as long as your arm of people who had very good reason to hate his guts. But which one actually did it?"

James put down his glass. "That is a question for another day. You have taken a little boy home to his mum and dad today, so let's be appreciative of that fact for a few hours at least and go to bed."

Chapter 54

Sharon left the interview room and walked out of the main doors onto Pitt Street. She needed some air. The detective walked to the coffee shop on the corner and bought a takeout cappuccino and double espresso, carrying them back to the station and taking the lift to the serious crime floor.

Dermot was seated at his desk when she set the cardboard cup down beside his laptop.

He looked up. “Thanks. Although I’m not sure what I’ve done to deserve it.”

“I needed to get out of the station after the interview with Kirsty Turner, it was pretty intense.”

Dermot lifted the cup and took a sip, grateful for the caffeine hit. He’d been scanning the information from the Orkney child abuse case for hours. His eyes felt gritty with tiredness. “I can imagine.”

“She’s got a decent lawyer. Her employers sent one of their best solicitors. But I’m not sure Kirsty will be fit to stand on trial for taking little Charlie. She seems to be having a complete breakdown.”

“I’m not surprised. The woman spent her formative years in the care system and she’s just found out she should have been with her real parents all along.” Dermot whistled. “It’s heavy stuff.”

Sharon nodded. “Kirsty told us she often watches families through their living room windows during her walk home from work. She likes to observe their routines and see the interaction between them.”

“She was obviously trying to fill a gap in her own life. I know she did a terrible thing in taking Charlie, but it’s a heart-breaking situation.”

“Apparently, Kirsty had seen Alice with Charlie a few times when she’d walked past. Alice and

Fergus's flat is on her route home. She'd become obsessed with them, I suppose. Then, she saw Alice and I at the building where she works, when we were interviewing the Earth's Saviours members. This only intensified her interest. She worked out we were police officers. I'm not surprised if Kirsty has some residual resentment towards us. A couple of PCs stood back and did nothing as she and her brother were dragged from their mother's arms."

"How did she find out what nursery Charlie went to?"

"On the evening when Alice left Charlie in the car for a few moments and Kirsty leant in to see if he was alright, she spotted his book bag on the seat beside him. It has the name of the nursery printed on it."

"These schools really do have a security problem." Dermot sighed.

"She watched Charlie playing in the playground at nursery from the street, waiting until pickup time. On a couple of occasions Alice was late to fetch him. Charlie was the last child there, looking upset."

"So, Kirsty decided she'd be the one to pick him up." Dermot knocked back the last of his espresso. "What was she planning to do? Why take Charlie out on the roof of that building if she cared so much for him?"

"Kirsty's mental health was unravelling. Once she had Charlie I think she panicked. The sedative kept him quiet whilst she could think what to do. I suppose she decided it was all too much. She may very well have intended to jump from the roof and take Charlie with her."

"I feel sorry for her, and for Alice and Fergus. But Kirsty should now receive psychiatric care. I cannot see any purpose in a prison sentence."

"Same here." Sharon shook her head wearily.

"Those officials involved in removing the children from their homes back in 2002 have a great deal to answer for. The impact is still being felt."

"Well, three of them are dead."

Sharon gestured towards his sheet of notes. "Have you identified anyone affected by the Orkney cases who could possibly have committed the murders?"

Dermot ran his finger along the scribbled text. "Other than the Turners, most of the families were reunited within a few months. From what I can tell, they've all gone on to live happy lives, far away from North Dorga. The Laughton children suffered a similar fate to Kirsty Turner – ending up in the care system and foster homes. But in the case of that family, the removal of the children was entirely justified. I can't see why they would have held a grudge against Lester or the social workers?"

"No, neither can I. The evidence seems to lead us back to the Turner family and Lester's own children. Ian was so affected by the details of his father's role in the affair that he cut all ties with his father and returned to North Dorga in an effort to make amends for what he'd done."

"And his sister has opted out of conventional life; changing her name and living a nomadic existence, never putting down ties, getting involved with the environmental movement." Dermot rested his head in his hand. "Billi Star had been to the Earth's Saviours offices a few times, hadn't she? I wonder if she knew Kirsty Turner worked in the same building. It seems a hell of a coincidence if she didn't?"

"Yes, Billi said she went there to help make banners and stuff, even if she wasn't keen on joining the organisation."

Sharon was considering this piece of information

when Klara approached the two officers.

"I'm sorry to interrupt, but I have received a call from my contact at Highlands and Islands police."

Dermot sat up straighter in his seat. "Oh yes?"

"They have now linked together the deaths of the two ladies and have re-opened the case into the death of Irene Vickers. As a result, they performed forensic tests on both of the teddy bears found near the bodies."

Dermot held his breath, hardly daring to hope for a piece of luck to come their way.

"They found a fingerprint on the ribbon of the bear that was placed under the fender of the white van that dragged Mrs Vickers to her death. It doesn't match anything recorded on the database, but it is now stored on file, nevertheless."

Dermot exhaled deeply. "At last! We have some forensic evidence from one of the crime scenes."

"When we have a suspect, we can perform a check," Sharon added. "Now, all we need to do is make an arrest."

Chapter 55

The streets of Glasgow were still eerily quiet. Dan Clifton had decided to walk from the train station to Pitt Street rather than taking the bus. He wanted to clear his head and have some time to think. The conference had three days left to run. Apparently, on the final day, there would be another huge gathering in George Square. But for now, the city lay silent with expectation.

He and Tyler had arrived back from North Dorga the previous evening and the DC had enjoyed a long, hot shower in his riverside flat. It seemed as if his body was covered in days' worth of mud and salty sea spray. He still felt as if he could identify the lingering reek of raw fish and diesel on his skin from the boat that took them from Dorga to Kirkwall, despite drowning himself in Calvin Klein that morning.

It had broken Dan's heart to receive the news that Hugh Turner's daughter had kidnapped Alice's little boy. It felt as if the poor family had been through enough. But when Hugh was informed, he demanded he be allowed to see his daughter at the police station. Kirsty had agreed and the man was now making his way to Glasgow, ready to meet his daughter after twenty years apart. The idea of this reunion made tears sting Dan's eyes. He swiftly brushed them away.

Before he knew it, the entrance doors to the Pitt Street headquarters were swinging open in front of him. He walked through them with a sense of determination.

*

The DCI approached Dan's desk as he pulled up his

chair and logged into the system. "Well done on your work in North Dorga. I realise it couldn't have been easy being stranded out there just the two of you. But the rapport you built with the locals enabled us to find out the full extent of the child abuse scandal."

"Thanks Ma'am. But it was you guys who uncovered the murders of the two social workers, that means we could be looking for a serial offender here. I wanted to get straight back onto the case, but I told Tyler to take a couple of days off. The trip to Dorga really took it out of him. I hope that's okay?"

Dani pulled up a chair. "Of course. I'm surprised you're back so soon, to be honest. But as you are, I'm grateful for your help. What were the feelings of the locals about what happened there twenty years ago? Did anyone seem angry enough to have sought revenge on such a scale?"

"To be honest, Ma'am, I think their approach was to keep it quiet. Dorga isn't a tourist hot-spot at the best of times and I reckon the whole incident is considered a blemish on their history. The DC based at the station on St Martin, Tracey Harvey, had been a schoolgirl on the island when it happened. Half her schoolmates were affected by the social services investigation, but she never uttered a single word to us about it. She hadn't even told her colleague, Eddie Shewan, who'd been based on the island for a decade. He had no idea himself about the place's turbulent past."

Dani sighed heavily. "It's not always such a good idea to brush these things under the carpet."

"Well, it's twenty years on and still no English settlers have returned. Whether the estate agents put them off, or the rumours still linger, I've no idea."

"Perhaps it would be better for the islanders to

meet the past head-on; create a memorial perhaps or issue an apology to the parents involved. This is sometimes the only way to move on."

Dan nodded solemnly. "The only person angry enough to kill was Hugh Turner and until now, he hasn't left the island since his kids were taken. I checked with the ferry boat company."

"He is due to arrive today. Kirsty Turner has been removed by the medical team to a secure hospital. Her father can visit her there. I expect she'll be under their care for some time."

"At least Hugh can finally have contact with her. I think he truly believed he'd never see either of his children again. How's Alice?"

"She's at home with Fergus and Charlie. They're both shaken up, of course. But very relieved Charlie is safe and there was no long lasting harm done."

Dan was about to ask if the department had organised for flowers to be sent to their flat when Sharon leapt to her feet at the next workstation.

"I think I've got something, Ma'am!"

Dani swivelled on her heels. "What is it?"

Sharon's voice had lifted an octave. "I spoke with the squad car keeping a surveillance on the house Billi Star is staying in. Apparently, she's not left it in the last day and is definitely inside, they've see her through the front window. Anyway, I thought I might run a check on the address, see who the friend is that Billi has persuaded to let her kip there." Sharon waved a sheet of paper she'd written a note down on. "The owner is named on the most recent council tax bill. It belongs to Todd McCleary!"

Dani creased her brow in confusion.

Sharon continued. "He's the manager of the woodland centre at the Argyll Forest, Ma'am. He's the one who told us Billi may have hung around with young Harry and the other wood workers. He didn't mention for one second that he *knew* who she was, let alone that she was staying in his *house*!"

Dani could finally see what her DS was getting so excited about. "You and Dermot need to get over there fast. Let's bring this guy in for the questioning. In the meantime, we will find out everything there is to know about Mr Todd McCleary."

Chapter 56

Darkness was falling as Dermot drove his car along the bumpy track towards the visitor centre in the depths of the Argyll Forest. The dense foliage was cutting out what remained of the light.

"We're a hell of a long way from Glasgow out here. Why would the manager have a house in the city? He couldn't possibly commute?"

Sharon shook her head. "He must stay out this way somewhere whilst he's working. The surveillance team say nobody else has come in or out of the house on Danes Drive except Billi in the last forty eight hours."

They climbed out of the car and approached the entrance doors. Sharon rattled the handle, but they were locked. She peered through the window. The interior was in darkness. "Shit. I didn't want to call ahead and give him a chance to make a run for it. But it seems he's not here anyway."

"It is out of season. They must close before dusk."

Sharon thought about Harry and the woodworkers' camp in the forest. "There's a hut about half a mile away where the lads turn the wood. They might just still be there. Perhaps they know where McCleary lives?"

"It's worth a try," Dermot replied.

Sharon tried to remember the route she and Alice had taken when they were there the week before. She strode through the avenue of silver birch trees until the trees became thicker and sturdier and the sky was eclipsed by their intertwined branches.

Dermot switched on the light on his phone. The weak beam didn't provide much illumination. Sharon concentrated hard, trying to recall the path she had taken previously. Her boots carefully navigating the roots protruding from the forest floor. The last thing they needed was for one of them to take a fall.

Finally, she spotted a flickering orange glow through the trees. It was a fire that had been set in the brazier by the wooden hut. Sharon released the breath she'd been holding with relief. Someone was still there.

She nudged Dermot's arm and pointed into the trees. "This is the camp they use."

The pair approached the clearing. Sharon paused when she heard voices up ahead. It sounded like an argument was taking place. She turned to Dermot, indicating they shouldn't make their presence known just yet. They stalked forward to the boundary of the copse, where they could make out the words being spoken but couldn't be easily seen.

Sharon recognised the figure of Todd McCleary, wearing the green jumper and corduroy slacks he'd had on when they last saw him. The man was remonstrating with one of the woodworkers, she recalled his name was Justin. There didn't seem to be anyone else there at the makeshift encampment.

Todd was standing a couple of feet away from the young man. "I promise you this is the truth! I want to get justice for you and your sister. Everything we have done is for you! Me and Billi Star, we've been taking direct action on your behalf. She's not been answering my calls the last few days, but the police have finally flushed her out, thanks to me. I'm sure she wants to see this thing through as much as I do, she's just had a touch of cold feet. We need to explain everything, for the sake of you and your sister!"

Justin was backing away from the older man, his face creased in confusion. "I don't know what you're talking about! I don't even have a sister! My older brother lives in Fife. My parents live in Helensburgh. My name is Justin Porter."

Todd shook his head in frustration. "Justin Sam Porter is the name you were given after your adoption. But your birth name is Sam Turner! You were taken from your family by social services on the 20th February 2002. But they never should have taken you away. The family did nothing wrong. I tried to tell my superiors what was happening, but nobody listened. In the end, the inspectors who led the inquiry into the debacle shook my hand for the information I'd given them, but what use was that to me? My bosses knew I'd given evidence against them and my life at work was a misery. I had to leave the job I loved. But worse than that, I had to live with the knowledge I'd failed you and your sister, and all the others they questioned in those little rooms. I sat there whilst the most awful things were being suggested to you. I did nothing!"

Justin was shaking his head, "I don't understand what you're talking about, Mr McCleary. Please just let me go!"

"I don't want to hurt you. That's the last thing I want. But I need to tell you the truth! I've punished them for you, the ones who took you away. The woman who dragged you out of your mother's arms – I made sure she suffered appropriately, dragged beneath the wheels of a fast vehicle, feeling her flesh being ripped from her bones! And the one who pulled your sister from the bathroom, where she'd desperately clung on to the sink – I drowned her in the bath. I would have done it in the sink but she was a big woman, she'd struggled too hard. The basin would've come away before I was finished."

Justin's eyes were wide with disbelief. "What are you telling me? Have you *killed* people?"

Todd reached out and grabbed the young man's arm. "I just need you to listen, that's all!"

Sharon and Dermot had heard enough. The DI made a sprint for the older man, wrestling him to the ground and tugging his hands behind his back. "Todd McCleary. I am arresting you for the murders of Mabel Flett and Irene Vickers. You do not have to say anything. But, it may harm your defence if you do not mention when questioned something which you later rely on in court. Anything you do say may be given in evidence."

Whilst Dermot read McCleary his rights, Sharon approached Justin and pulled him aside. "Are you okay, did he hurt you?"

The young man shook his mop of blond hair. "No, I'm fine. But those things he was saying? Please tell me it was all bullshit? Surely the man is just a lunatic?"

Sharon sighed heavily. "I'm sorry Justin, but some of the things he said were very probably the truth. We will be taking you back to our headquarters in Glasgow, if you agree? We will want you to make a statement about what you just heard. Someone there will be able to explain it all properly. We'll make sure you have your parents and a counsellor with you."

Chapter 57

All three interview rooms were full. Dani Bevan had been watching the footage from each on the bank of monitors in the media suite. Finally, a break had been called and Dani could exit the stuffy room and return to the open-plan office floor.

Andy got up from his desk to meet her. "Can I make you a cuppa? How is it going?"

"Yes please." She dropped into the swivel chair Dan usually occupied, rubbing her face with her hands, closing her eyes for a moment.

Andy came back from the trolley with a mug of coffee, straight from the machine.

"Thanks, I need this." She took a long sip, the drink was lukewarm but still welcome. "Justin Porter has finished making his statement. Fortunately, his recall of what McCleary told him was very good. It matches the recording we have from Dermot's phone."

"Good, but that recording was very faint from what I heard. Will it be allowed in court?" Andy frowned.

"We're getting a transcript written up. Alongside Justin's testimony, we should be able to use it. Although, McCleary is certainly not confessing now. He's denied the two charges of murder and his brief has recommended a 'no comment' interview."

"We still need some forensic evidence then?"

Dani nodded. "A swab has been taken from both McCleary and Billi Star for a DNA analysis. We have both their fingerprints. They are being checked against the fingerprint on the teddy bear in Inverness as we speak."

"What do we have on Billi Star?"

"Sharon is interviewing her. She claims Todd McCleary is just a friend who lets her stay in his house in Glasgow from time to time. It was pointed out that it is something of a coincidence he also happened to be the social worker who blew the whistle on her father, Mabel Flett and Irene Vickers twenty years ago. She just smiled." Dani felt her chest tighten at the memory of the woman's smug face.

"Everything we've got against Billi Star is circumstantial. Do you really think she's involved in the murders?"

Before Dani had a chance to answer, Klara Laska approached them. "I hope you don't mind, but as my contract has a few more hours to run, I thought I would continue to do some research into Todd McCleary."

The DCI put down her mug. "Great, what have you got?"

Klara leant her weight on the edge of the desk. "The name of the whistle-blower in the child abuse scandal on North Dorga was never mentioned in the crown investigation report to protect their identity. But I can see from their personnel records, seized by Highlands and Islands police this afternoon, that Todd McCleary was a junior social worker for Caithness and South Orkney Council from 1999-2003. He worked in the Golspie offices, alongside Flett and Vickers. He resigned in October 2003."

"We don't have any proof McCleary was the one who gave evidence against his colleagues, but his employment records certainly indicate he was there at the time and if we add that to what he said to Justin Porter in the forest, I think we can be sure it was him."

Klara nodded. "It seems that after he left the job in Golspie, he performed some voluntary work for a while, before getting his first job at Woodland Scotland in the Bilbster Forest, Caithness. He started out as a guide, but got promoted to managing one of the visitors centres in 2010. He moved to the job at the Argyll Forest five years ago. There is a small bungalow in the grounds that the manager lives in rent free. So, at some point he was able to buy a property in Glasgow. With a bit more digging, I can find out when."

"This is excellent work, Klara. We can connect him to both the eastern Highlands and to Glasgow, where all our murders were committed. But what we really need to know, is how McCleary and Billi Star met one another. How did they get so close Billi could use his house as her own. Did they plan this entire programme of revenge between them?" Dani sighed.

Dan Clifton approached his colleagues from the lift, his shift just starting. "I can give Ian Lester a call, Ma'am? Find out if he knows anything else about his sister's movements in the last few years, maybe call the mother too. They might just tell us something new?"

"Yes please, Dan. Find out everything, even the most trivial detail. The lives of these two must have overlapped at some point. Now," she got to her feet. "I need to get back to the media room to observe these interviews. Let's hope Sharon and Dermot can get us *something* we can use against them."

Chapter 58

Andy watched his boss leave the department, deep in his own thoughts. As the lift doors slid closed, he turned to Klara on the next desk. "This 'Woodland Scotland' that McCleary works for, you'd describe it as an environmental charity, wouldn't you?"

Klara glanced up from her screen. "Yes, although is also gets government funding. That's mentioned on it's website."

Andy rolled his chair in closer. "Then wouldn't they be sending delegates to COP26? I mean, if a charity protecting Scotland's woodland wasn't represented at the climate conference, it would be a bit of an oversight, wouldn't it?"

Klara's mouth dropped open. She didn't reply, but went onto the COP26 official website and performed a quick search. "Well I'll be damned. Woodland Scotland certainly *did* have a delegate present at the conference this year. He attended a series of lectures and discussion groups at the SEC on the third day."

"That's the day Quentin Lester was murdered."

Klara swivelled ninety degrees to face him. "And guess who their delegate was for that day?"

"Todd McCleary."

*

Dermot had been called out of the interview room just before lunch. If he was honest, he'd needed a break. Much as he wanted to be the one to drum the truth out of McCleary, the man was proving a tough nut to crack. His solicitor was obviously good and he'd got nothing from him but a barrage of 'no comments', for the previous few hours.

As he reached the serious crime floor, he was surprised to see a group of his colleagues waiting eagerly for his arrival. "What's all this?"

Andy stepped forward. "Sorry to interrupt your interview, but we thought you'd want to hear this piece of information."

Klara got up from her desk. "I've just been speaking with the security team at the SEC. They have forwarded me all the attendance records for the 1st November."

"The day Lester was killed?" Dermot added.

Klara nodded. "On that day, Todd McCleary attended every single lecture and a couple of focus group meetings as the delegate of Woodland Scotland. One of the security officers down there is checking CCTV right now for any images of him that day. In fact, he was in one of the same seminar groups as Quentin Lester during that morning."

Dermot's eyes widened. "Holy Smoke. We can place McCleary in the same building as Lester on the day he was killed!"

Andy raised his hand, as if to lessen his colleague's expectations. "Yes, we can, especially with CCTV footage. But the registers show McCleary was present in an afternoon seminar straight after lunch. Looking at the timeframe of the murder, it doesn't seem possible McCleary could have gone back to Lester's hotel room, committed the crime and got back for his meeting at 12.45pm."

Dermot felt the sudden urge to scream. "It's all bloody circumstantial!"

Dan put down the phone on his desk and came to join them. "I've just been speaking with Lester's ex-wife. She claims that when she found out her husband's role in the North Dorga child abuse scandal, back in 2001, she was disgusted. She's been ashamed about it ever since and never mentions it to anyone. Fiona Lester, now Black, filed for divorce within weeks. She moved away with their two children. She claims she tried to protect them from the worst of the details, but Elinor was nearly thirteen at the time and the internet was just getting started. According to her, Elinor Lester, now calling herself Billi Star, became obsessed with the case her father had been involved in. She collected newspaper reports and constantly searched online for updates. At one point, Fiona took her daughter to a child psychologist, but it didn't seem to do much good."

"So, Billi Star knew all about the fate of the Turner family, the role of her father in the sorry affair, *and* that of Mabel Flett and Irene Vickers," Dermot said. "She would also have known there was a whistle-blower, but not their name probably, as it wasn't in the public domain."

"In the end, Fiona became sick of it. She wanted to leave her ex-husband in the past and any memory of what he did. She said Ian was interested in the events, but only up to a point. Her daughter, on the other hand, went completely off the rails. She failed her Highers and dropped out of school. Fiona lost track of her soon after. She was living in Colinton then with her new husband and says her daughter drops by every so often, or calls, but that's it."

"It's desperately sad, really," Klara noted.

Dan continued. "It got me thinking. If Billi Star was so obsessed with the child abuse case, maybe she joined some online forums and stuff? That's where these people fixated on real crime hang out, isn't it? I think we should do an Internet search, see what turns up?"

"It's certainly worth a try, we've got McCleary's phone and laptop and Billi's phone for the time being. The techies are trawling them as we speak," Dermot said despondently. "We've nothing else solid to go on until the forensic results come back. I've applied for an extension to hold McCleary for another thirty six hours, which we should be granted as we're looking at a multiple murder charge. Billi however, will be set free at 4pm. We've not got enough to charge her with anything right now."

"Then we'll need to get a bloody move on, won't we?" Dan dropped into his chair and pulled a laptop towards him. The others did the same.

Chapter 59

The street was busy with parked cars. Andy eventually found a space several houses along. He let out a laugh as Sharon tried to clamber out of the passenger seat with a huge bouquet of flowers in her arms.

"Don't just stand there laughing, give me a bloody hand, would you?"

Andy took the bouquet as his friend stepped onto the pavement and adjusted her top.

They walked together in silence up to the front door of the ground floor flat. Andy pressed the bell, just hoping they would be welcome visitors.

He decided he needn't have worried. Alice answered the door with a beaming smile on her face and Charlie sitting contentedly on her hip.

"Hey, there! Do come in. I just put the kettle on for you."

"Music to our ears," Sharon said cheerily, following her colleague inside.

"Wow, what a lovely flat. Really full of character!" Andy said genuinely.

Alice placed her son on the thick rug in the centre of the living room floor. Wooden toys were placed all around him. She stood up and took the flowers from Andy. "They're gorgeous, thank you."

"It a gift from the whole department. It's not much, just a little token." Andy looked embarrassed.

"I'm really grateful. Fergus will love them too. It's good to know our friends are thinking of us."

Sharon went out to find a vase.

"Is Fergus back at work?" Andy asked.

"Yep, he couldn't stay away much longer without having to hand over his case to another lawyer. To be honest, I wanted to get Charlie back into his old routine as soon as possible. He has no clue what happened to him, so I don't want to impose my worries onto the little guy. He really needs to go back to nursery soon, but I don't think I could ever set foot in his old place. Just the thought brings me out in a sweat."

"I can totally understand that." Andy reached into his pocket and handed her a crisp business card. "Carol asked me to give you this. It's the details for the nursery she works at. I know it's a bit further away from here, but it's actually not that far from Pitt Street. It's a busy place but really well run and Carol says if Charlie was to go there, she'd keep a special eye on him. There's no way he'd be picked up by anyone other than you or Fergus, that's for sure."

Alice took the card, suddenly finding there were tears running down her cheeks. "God, I'm really sorry. It's just that this is such a wonderful relief. To think Charlie could attend a nursery where someone as lovely as Carol would be looking after him." She fished a tissue from her pocket and dabbed her eyes.

"No need to apologise. I totally understand. Amy went to the same nursery where Carol worked because we were so worried about her being away from us that young. We're all the same when it comes to our kiddies."

Sharon re-entered the room with a tray full of coffees, she set them down on the low table. "Your flowers are in a vase by the sink. You can choose where to put them later." She noticed Alice's damp face and the balled up tissue in her hand. "Has Andy been upsetting you? I can take him home again if you like?"

Alice laughed. "No, you're okay. He's grand."

They all took a seat. Andy handed out the mugs.

"Now," Alice said eagerly. "You must tell me how the investigation is going. It's been killing me not knowing what's happening."

It was Sharon who answered. "You will know that Kirsty Turner has been detained in a psychiatric hospital for the time being?" She eyed her colleague cautiously, unsure what her reaction would be to this news.

"Yes, I was told. I know she'll probably stay there for the foreseeable future. The woman is ill, she needs treatment. Of course I'm angry with her, but I can recognise that. What about her father? Has he made contact?"

"I believe he's visited her a few times. It's going to take a long time to rebuild their relationship, but it's a start. Social services confirmed that Justin Porter was indeed the youngest Turner child. He was formally adopted in 2003 and received a new name. He genuinely has no memory of his birth family, even though he was eight when he was removed from them."

"A bet it's a reaction to the trauma. The poor kid probably blanked it out of his mind. How is he taking the news now?"

"He's seeing a counsellor. There's been some talk of him meeting his father at some point in the future, but they're not sure the lad is quite ready yet," Andy sipped his drink thoughtfully.

"But he's probably less damaged than Kirsty," Alice noted. "Because he had such a stable upbringing. She was the one who remembered it all and was shifted from pillar to post during her childhood."

There was a moment's silence as they contemplated this fact.

Eventually, Sharon said, "the boss is charging Todd McCleary today."

Alice shuffled forward. This was the information she really wanted to hear.

"Two counts of murder. The confession he made to Justin in the woods has been corroborated by the recording made on Dermot's phone. An expert has decided it's more than ninety percent likely to be McCleary's voice, plus they've got Justin's testimony. The fingerprint on the teddy's ribbon was a match for his, plus he had no alibis for the days the two women were killed. Klara even found he'd booked into a hotel in Inverness the night before Irene Vickers' murder. The Fiscal's office said there was enough evidence to bring charges. We will just have to hope it's enough for a jury."

"What about the murder of Quentin Lester? That was our case after all?"

Sharon sighed heavily. "McCleary is clearly shown on CCTV at the SEC canteen at the exact time Lester was being murdered in his hotel room."

Alice shook her head in puzzlement.

Andy took up the story, "we found several online forums where the Orkney child abuse cases were being discussed. Some of the contributors seemed to have insider information on the cases, so we assume a few must have worked for the police or social services. Todd McCleary was named in a number of threads as the whistle-blower. We found Billi Star had accessed two of these sites from her mobile phone in recent years. We think she contacted McCleary and explained who she was. How Lester was her father and she wanted him to pay for what he did. They became friends; united by an obsession with the same awful misuse of power that the child abuse scandal had been."

"But is there proof of this?"

"Sadly, the proof is flimsy. There's an email thread between Billi and McCleary going back a couple of years. But they are careful not to discuss anything controversial in them. It's more about times and places to meet. Billi's fingerprints are all over McCleary's place in Scotstoun so she must have stayed there a lot. There's no doubt they discussed more sensitive stuff in private. They both must have tracked down the Turner children. McCleary knew the details of the boy's adoption as the wheels had been put in motion before he left his job in Golspie. He then approached Justin, who had trained in woodwork at a college in Helensburgh, and offered him the workshop in the Argyll forest a year ago in return for some manual work felling trees. Justin says he jumped at the chance, didn't ask too many questions about it."

"Billi discovered Kirsty was working in the same building as the Earth's Saviours headquarters. She didn't care much for the organisation, but by dropping by every so often, she could keep her eye on the woman working on the floor below. It probably also gave her the idea of using the cross as a murder weapon. Because we are now pretty damn sure it was *Billi* who killed her father, not Todd McCleary."

Chapter 60

Sharon finished her coffee and placed the empty mug on a coaster. "Yes, we think it was Billi Star who killed Quentin Lester. It was McCleary who had the biggest gripe against his ex-colleagues, Mabel and Irene. But Billi had hated her father. We think McCleary recognised Lester at the conference that day and couldn't believe his luck. They'd probably been waiting for an opportunity like this one, where their clever staging could reach a wide audience. It would also confuse anyone investigating the crime, who would assume the murder had something to do with COP26."

"So, you think McCleary contacted his friend Billi, to share the news her father was present at the SEC and very probably staying in a hotel nearby?" Alice suggested.

"Yep, although whatever phones they used to communicate with are probably now at the bottom of the Clyde," Andy said with disgust.

"We think Billi went to the conference centre and waited outside. We have to assume she knew her Dad's mobile number and gave him a call. That must have been the call Lester received on his phone from a pay-as-you-go number just after 12pm. She probably asked him to meet her during the lunchbreak, maybe suggested she was ready to reconcile. This would explain the twenty minutes or so we couldn't account for. Then they returned to his hotel room. I don't think Lester would have taken a stranger back there. He mustn't have thought his daughter posed a threat."

"She must have acted quickly, having her props concealed somewhere under that big black coat. She stabbed her father in the chest with the cross and as he was dying, she put the academic gown round his shoulders and pulled down his trousers," Andy explained. "She knew the cross and gown were items used to condemn the parents in the child abuse cases on North Dorga. She wanted to send us a message. Billi didn't manage to hit his vital organs but then she was in a hurry and had never killed anyone before. Luckily for her, daddy dearest had an advanced heart condition that did for him instead. Seeing your own daughter plunging a stake into your chest must be a mightily stressful experience."

Alice sat back in her chair, Charlie toddling up and placing his arms around her legs. "But you're telling me this can't be proven?"

Andy shook his head solemnly. "Nope. The hotel CCTV footage is inconclusive, although the experts say it fits with Billi's general height and build. She must have worn gloves throughout as there were no forensic traces in the room or on the weapon. McCleary is refusing to implicate her and simply because she hated her dad and doesn't have an alibi isn't enough to bring charges."

Alice puffed out her cheeks. "The DCS must be livid. The murder will be made public now and he hasn't got an arrest to placate the First Minister. It's a public relations disaster!"

Sharon and Andy exchanged meaningful glances.

"What is it?" Alice lifted her son onto her lap and narrowed her eyes suspiciously. "Come on, there's something you're not telling me."

"Dermot got in contact with some of his old mates in the security services. Apparently, for the duration of COP26, because of the high-level security code of some of the attendees -,"

"Yeah, like the President of the United States," Alice spluttered.

Sharon nodded. "Well, it turns out the procedure in these circumstances is to designate the entire area as under the rule of the Official Secrets Act, 1989. For the entire duration of the conference. So that nobody can then be tempted to let slip the whereabouts of somebody super-important."

Unexpectedly, Alice started to laugh. Her whole body was shaking with mirth. Charlie looked at her in surprise, then joined in himself, clapping his hands together with glee at the joke. When she had finally regained some composure she said, "So, the DCS has a prime excuse to cover the entire thing up? I don't believe it!"

Andy shrugged his shoulders, as if he'd seen it all before and this was another example of the higher-ups getting what they wanted. "We kept the details as closely guarded as we could, anyway. But everyone in the team, including yourself, plus any witnesses we interviewed in relation to the murder, will have to come into the station and sign the 1989 act in relation to this incident. Basically, if they tell anyone else about it, they'll get banged up."

Alice was still shaking her head. "I don't bloody believe it! But what about Billi Star? You think she's a cold blooded killer, but she'll walk away from this and nobody will even know the murder happened?"

Sharon grimaced. "That's about the size of it. Lester hadn't re-married. He had no friends outside of work and his colleagues were indifferent to him. His family didn't care if he lived or died. There won't be anyone asking any questions about how he met his end. Besides, his official death certificate will read that he died of a massive heart attack."

Alice eyes were wide with wonder. "Fergus hinted to me that these sorts of cover-ups happened occasionally, but I don't think I really believed him, you know?" She gazed into the smiling face of her son. “I suppose it ties everything up rather neatly, doesn’t it? There’s only one problem really.”

Andy collected together the used mugs and put them on the tray, ready to take them into the kitchen to be washed up. “Yes, we just have to hope to God that Billi Star doesn’t decide she’s got a taste for it and sets out to kill again.”

“Precisely,” Alice replied, her tone as cold as ice.

Chapter 61

DCI Dani Bevan walked out of the office and closed the door gently behind her. She'd just attended the most high-level meeting of her career. The DCC, the DCS and the First Minister herself were in attendance.

Teas and coffees were handed around by one of the canteen assistants but Dani found the hot liquid nearly made her choke. But it turned out it was the accompanying chit-chat that was hardest to swallow.

The First Minister was congratulating her senior officers on the success of the climate conference. The smoothness of the transport routes were praised and the policing of the largely peaceful demonstrations which were so much a symbol of their great democratic nation. Dani shook hands with everyone in the room. She maintained a pleasant expression and accepted the glowing accolades heaped upon her own team. At least DCS Douglas had the decency not to quite manage eye contact with her.

At the earliest possible opportunity, Dani had made her excuses and left. Now, the walk back to the serious crime floor seemed interminable. Her entire team were going to be there to welcome her return. She had always prided herself on never giving up on an open investigation. Her tenacity had always got results in the past. But in this particular instance, when she saw the expectant faces of her loyal and hardworking team, for the first time in her career, Dani knew she would be entirely lost for words.

The End

If you enjoyed this novel, please take a few moments to write a brief review. Reviews really help to introduce new readers to my books and this allows me to keep on writing.
Many thanks,

Katherine.

If you would like to find out more about my books and read my reviews and articles then please visit my blog, TheRetroReview at:

www.KatherinePathak.wordpress.com

To find out about new releases and special offers follow me on Twitter:

@KatherinePathak

Most of all, thanks for reading!

If you enjoyed this book, have you read the others in the DCI Dani Bevan series?

Against A Dark Sky

Book 1 in the DCI Dani Bevan series

They died thirty years ago, but the case is not closed...

Five walkers set out to climb Ben Lomond on a fine October day. Within hours, the weather has taken a turn for the worst. The group find themselves lost on the mountain. Two of the climbers manage to make it back down and call for help.
The following day a body is found. One of the female climbers has been strangled and another man is missing without trace.
DCI Dani Bevan is called to the Loch Lomond town of Ardyle to lead the case. It quickly becomes clear that Bevan must dig into the events of a similar tragedy which occurred on the hills thirty years earlier in order to find the killer.
This investigation requires the DCI to face up to the ghosts of her own tragic past, and to endeavour to put them behind her, once and for all.

On A Dark Sea

Book 2 in the DCI Dani Bevan series

A missing girl.

A broken marriage.

Who can you trust?

When fourteen year old Maisie Riddell goes missing from a Glasgow High School, DCI Dani Bevan knows she needs to act fast, particularly as the Headmistress is the wife of her DS, Phil Boag. But as the inquiry into the girl's disappearance deepens, Bevan finds herself caught in the fall-out from a broken marriage, unsure of whose word she can really trust. The DCI is required to take her search to Norway, in order to discover the truth about Maisie's secret life.

Meanwhile, Bill Hutchison's unauthorised investigation into a brutal murder in Stonehaven places him in terrible danger. With Dani wrapped up in the Riddell case, who is there left to help him...?

A Dark Shadow Falls

Book 3 in the DCI Dani Bevan series

Never invite evil into your home...

DCI Dani Bevan finds herself dragged into the disturbing case of Eric Fisher, a man accused of slaughtering his own family in a case of domestic homicide. But when a spate of violent burglaries breaks out in the area, whilst Fisher is on remand, Dani wonders if the man's claims of innocence are as crazy as they first thought.
The DCI quickly becomes caught up in a race against time to stop a terrifying serial killer, who appears to be one step ahead of Dani's every move.

A Dark Shadow Falls is perhaps the darkest of all the DCI Bevan investigations. It is a police procedural which uncovers dark secrets and a deadly obsession with the bloodiest episodes in Scottish history.

Printed in Great Britain
by Amazon